Rainbows in April

To Dorothy

All Blessings

Moyra Mayo

Rainbows in April is dedicated to my children, Angela and Stephen, and my grandchildren, Lydia and Reuben. Without their love, support and constant encouragement, this book would not have been published.

Rainbows in April
by
Moya Mayo

Published in association with
Limelight Classic Productions Ltd

Limelight

www.limelightclassics.com

Published in 2013 by Limelight Classic Productions Limited

Copyright © Moya Mayo 2013

All rights reserved

The moral rights of the author have been asserted

No part of this book may be reproduced or transmitted in any form or any means without written permission from the copyright holder, except by a reviewer who may quote brief passages in connection with a review for insertion in a newspaper, magazine, website, or broadcast

British Library Cataloguing in Publication Data:
A catalogue record for this book is available from the British Library

ISBN-13: 9780956039231

Printed & bound in North Shields by
yourPrintDepartment.co.uk

Limelight Classic Productions Ltd
Fort House
Old Hartley
NE26 4RL

Chapter I

The late afternoon sun slipped from behind a light cloud. As if by magic, the rain stopped and steam began to rise from the drying pavements. The momentary April shower vanished as quickly as it had come, as if it had made way for something else in the sky.

It was 1944 and the Second World War was at its height and Britain was taking a battering. The constant air raids had been designed to seep the country of its courage. Instead, they had strengthened the back-bone of the populace which rose to the occasion of its nation's needs.

The sudden dreaded wail of the air raid siren told an instantly alert city that the Luftwaffe were on their way. From all directions, people streamed towards the shelters. Mothers, grannies, aunts and a lesser number of men carrying gas masks, bedding, candles and the ever ready bags of food-stuffs, all struggled with children towards the safety of the underground shelters. The warning had hardly died away when the threatening grumbles of the approaching bombers could be heard.

A young woman in naval uniform quickened her steps. Two sailors caught up with her and the three looked around at the now empty street. An ARP Warden, about to close the door of the shelter, saw them, and urged them to hurry. As the bombers neared, the sailors grabbed an arm each and lifted the young woman off her feet and through the iron door. It clanked behind them and they found themselves stumbling in the dim light, struggling towards the wider section of the underground shelter.

As the door clanged behind them, the first of the bombs landed and the earth shuddered. The three found a corner into which they settled down and introduced themselves. The elder of the two sailors, Stan Bailey was from the North East of England. His mate, Joe Baxter was from Wales. The girl was Rose Bamber and she told them she had no roots anywhere. Her father had been an army man who had dragged his wife and child from country to country. Thus it was that Rose found herself quite naturally able to speak foreign languages.

Games with her father had really been lessons in geography. His vast knowledge of travel abroad, his interest in trains and their routes, had all been part of his idea of play with his only child. All this of course was of interest to her superiors, thus it was that Rose, although poorly schooled, had found herself accepted in the WRENS and given the job of driving top brass from base to base. Her knowledge of languages was also useful for interpreting the many and varied bits of information which came the way of various sections.

Joe fell asleep. Stan hitched himself along as much as he could. He and Rose had talked most of the night. He felt that he knew the girl better than any other he had met. There was a fragility about her, a gentleness, and at the same time, her lovely, deep eyes held an openness that struck him. In those eyes he saw something else, an uncertainty, a *need*. Perhaps she loved someone and wanted him now. Stan grinned; this dim shelter was getting to him, the sooner they were out of it the better.

For her part, Rose, having half lain and half sat all through the raid, looked at Stan without experiencing the least feeling of being a stranger. Rose gave him a glance and realised he was naturally kind and had a sense of humour.

He had told her of his father's little printing works in Hexham and could not wait for the war to end so he could return home and settle down to the family business. He had plans and, although he suspected the old man might take some persuading, he would still probably have to agree in the end. Rose summed up Stan as having a lovely nature and the courage of his convictions. She liked him, felt at ease with him and hoped his war would be a safe one.

Further down in the shelter, local people were enjoying a gossip. A granny with her charge strapped to her chest, comforted him.

'Never you mind little chuck. Your old gran won't let nobody harm you. None of us down 'ere are scared of them old ones...'

She glanced around her group.

...'Are we girls? Not bleedin' likely, anyway, just who the 'ell do 'ee think 'ee is? Bleedin' Hitler, I know what I'd like to do to 'im. I 'eard as 'ow 'ee was born in a back street in Austria. Should've tossed 'im out wiv the bath water. Bleedin' little Corporal from Gawd knows where.'

Suddenly, another much heavier boom rumbled through the shelter. For a moment there was silence, then the ARP Warden spoke.

'Bit close for comfort that was, blimey, listen to that.'

A building had collapsed somewhere above them. The shuddering rumble caused the children to whimper and the adults glanced at each other meaningfully.

A cheery grandmother suggested they had a sing-along to which they agreed:

I wish I was-s-s your boogie woogie bear.
I wish I was-s-s your boogie woogie bear.
If I was your boogie woogie bear,
You'd take me with you everywhere.
I wish I was-s-s your boogie woogie bear.

Within seconds, the shelter was filled with the sound of men, women and children all singing lustily. Their world outside might be falling apart, but down in the safety of the shelter, they sang their hearts out. The boogie woogie bear changed to doll, ball, chick, indeed anything which would fit the tune. From all quarters, there was laughter, and voices called out their choice, everyone making sure that each child had a turn at choosing.

The clarion sound of the 'All Clear' was heard from outside. Gathering themselves and their families together, the adults made an orderly line and they filed out into the light grey morning air, where firemen and ARP Wardens scurried about and a loud-speaker boomed out:

> 'WILL EVERYONE FROM THIS STREET PLEASE GO TO THE CHURCH CRYPT IN THE NEXT ROAD. THIS AREA HAS TO BE MADE SAFE.'

The warning was given repeatedly and Rose, along with Stan and Joe, followed the murmuring crowd. As the groups hurried along, they cast sideways glances at their homes. Ethel, the grandmother, still with her charge strapped to her, stopped mid-stride, gripped by horror as she stared in a trance at a gaping space in the middle of the terrace. A direct hit had completely demolished the house. Only the grey mists rising from the masonry were the ghostly remains of what, only yesterday, had been the home of at least three generations.

A near neighbour, and obviously close friend, confirmed that Ethel's house had gone. Her tone changed and she put an arm around her stricken friend. Her words came naturally, as they did so often in those days of war.

'Don't worry Ethel. What's a few sticks and stones anyway? You still got your family and you got me. You know love, what I got you can share. Tell you what, you and little Jimmy can move in wiv me.'

So saying, Ethel's friend and saviour guided her towards the church crypt.

'As you know, my two lads are at sea. My Ron, well he seems to live in that fire engine he drives. When we get sorted, just you come home and stay wiv us for the duration.'

Rose, Stan and Joe were in the crypt and each marvelled at the cheerfulness of everyone around. Right down one wall stood a row of trestle tables. Huge tea urns steamed and cups of tea, six at a time, were filled from massive teapots. Smiling, friendly ladies chattered to all and sundry as they worked. A friendly lady in WVS uniform told the three friends to find themselves seats as queues took second place to members of the armed services. Joe suddenly winked at

Stan and nodded towards a slim girl in the uniform of a nurse.

'Look mate, I'll see you at the gang plank. Always had a soft spot for the nurses.'

He rose, shrugged and grinned at Rose then turned and made straight for the nurse.

'Don't forget boyo, time and tide,' Stan called after him. The last they saw of Joe was his arm raised in a backward wave.

Stan looked at Rose and asked her how much time off she had. Rose sighed and confirmed that she had exactly twenty-four hours. She looked at her watch and said that she had to report for duty at six o'clock the following morning. Again she sighed. It was warm and cheerful in the crypt. She had spent the last twenty-four hours looking up the parents of a friend. The family, however, had moved away. Rose wondered how it was that a daughter would not know of such an important family event. Still, in war-time, such things happened. Letters were often not delivered and she had another twenty-four hours of freedom, which she intended to enjoy and, hopefully with Stan, if he had as much time as she did. She smiled at him and he grinned back, looking hopeful.

He leaned forward. 'Guess what?'

She shook her head and he winked.

'Twenty-four hours. SNAP.'

They looked at each other and his voice was soft as he whispered, 'Let's enjoy those hours Rose, let's just forget about the war, be ourselves for a few hours. What do you say?'

She took hold of Stan by the arm, looked at him, and nodded happily. Again, Stan saw an expression in her deep blue eyes. It seemed to hold him and he couldn't fathom what it was or what it meant. All he knew at that moment was, this girl suddenly meant a great deal to him. They'd known each other only twelve hours – was it really possible that he had fallen in love with her?

Rose glanced at him as he grinned. 'Going potty I think, all that time underground in a shelter, you know how sailors are, we like to see God's blue sky above us.'

She was overwhelmed at how he had looked after her and how sincere and caring he was, especially since he hardly knew her. She felt so at ease with him and wondered if this could be love. He tucked her arm in his more firmly and, as his face turned towards her, she stared into his caring eyes and knew they were stealing her heart away.

She smiled and nodded in the direction of the toilets.

'See you in a moment, then we'll give ourselves a time to remember.'

Later, walking through the battered streets, they talked. The earlier feelings of closeness strengthened, they strolled for miles, not knowing or caring where they were, except that they were together. The morning wore on, the rush hour became evident and they carried on talking. At last they reached a small café and went in.

The waitress was dashing about trying to serve everyone and apologised for there not being any bread that morning.

'It's buns or nothing. It's the baker you see,' she sniffed on a half sob. 'The poor man, he lost 'is wife last night in that raid. She was one of the best bakers for miles and he's come back to the ovens but no bread for at least an hour. Isn't he just wonderful?'

With a sigh, she carried on and both Rose and Stan enjoyed a hearty breakfast.

They left the café and came across a museum. It was one of those old specialist printing shops which catered for those with an interest in ancient writings and the earliest printing machines. Happily, Stan informed Rose of the intricacies of the subject he had been brought up with.

They went down a stone staircase which turned out to be an underground vault. There were no windows and only a few bits of machinery standing about. In a far corner, Rose noticed a tent-like cover. She was amazed to find that the tent had a mattress, a pillow, blankets and a large bag of flasks, foodstuffs and a bottle of rum.

Stan walked over after inspecting an ancient machine.

'Those two old dears upstairs are certainly on the ball, they've taken the "Be Prepared" order to heart,' he smiled,

Rose laughed and they agreed to go back upstairs. She made for the steps and, as she passed close to him, he suddenly reached for her. Drawing her as near to him as he could, he kissed her. At first it was a light kiss, then, looking down into her eyes, he kissed her again. This time it was a lover's kiss – an urgent call to her very being. Rose responded with all the pent up feeling of hours of waiting. At last, gasping, they stood apart.

'Let's get out of here before I take advantage of you,' he muttered.

They smiled at each other and in unison whispered, 'I love you.'

Again, they kissed

'Marry me, please Rose. We can do it, let's get a licence. In an hour you can be my wife,' whispered Stan.

Rose closed her eyes, then in a breathless voice replied, 'Yes, oh yes, Stan. Let's get married.'

Grabbing her by the hand, they made for the stone steps. Then suddenly, with a slow grinding sound, the door at the top crashed down the steps. Machines suddenly lurched halfway through the ceiling. Grey dust rose in a blinding mist, and the terrible sound of falling masonry above, told of yet another unexpected day-time raid. Clinging to each other, Rose and Stan staggered back to the wall. They watched in horror as the ceiling began to collapse. The sheer weight of the ancient machinery in the room above forced the now badly damaged floor on which it stood, to give way. With a sickening lurch, two more stout iron legs burst through just above their heads. With a dried terrified scream, Rose shrank back, edging herself along the wall like a trapped animal. Stan carefully followed her then gently put his arms around her.

The rumble from above stopped and an eerie silence hung in the air. The ancient, iron door from the entrance to the cellar now lay across what was left of the shattered stone steps. Only the grey rising dust was able to find an escape to the world outside. They were trapped in an underground world, with no way out except for the gap high up in the wall where the door had been. Stan studied the situation and agreed that they dared not move for fear of setting off further collapse by the already weakened ceiling above.

The tent had been placed quite obviously in the safest place, no machinery hung above it, and the ceiling seemed to be solid enough. Stan thought that perhaps the two old dears who ran the museum had set up this place in case they were unable to get out to the shelters.

He looked at Rose and winked.

'Let's get into that tent, I don't think there's going to be any more disturbance just now, come on.'

Rose looked at Stan and the sheer happiness she'd felt earlier had soon turned to terror. That was now subsiding but the fear of their situation was still with her. Was the love that they had just found ever going to see the sun? They were buried, not just in a cellar, but in an underground vault, way below any level they could expect others to know about. A dry sob ached her throat; quickly she sniffed and gave a little cough.

'I've heard about fast workers like you, telling a girl you love her one minute, then pulling her into a tent the next.' Stan grinned but his voice was serious as he spoke. 'Don't worry petal, I'll look after you, I'm going to do that for the rest of my life so I might as well get into practice.'

They then looked at each other and her eyes seemed like twin seas; in their depths Stan yet again saw the expression he'd seen earlier. This time he recognised it and his heart leapt - for it was love. He knew in that moment, that whatever might happen in the future, those twin seas would forever hold a fascination and a hold on his heart. He would love this girl forever.

Chapter II

He carefully felt for the zip of the tent. At least inside it would be dust free. At last, they were settled down and Rose poured out two mugs of tea from one of the flasks and, as if they were on a picnic, they happily munched biscuits. Time seemed to stand still and there was not much point in trying to escape – it would be far better to wait until help came. If they were to move about they might just put themselves in further danger so they felt the sensible thing to do was lie doggo.

Tentatively, Stan touched the sleeping bag and suggested they try and get some sleep but Rose would only agree if Stan got in with her. Her heart was beating fast and she felt a little breathless. If this were to be their last hours on earth, at least they would be close. Rose wasn't sure how far she meant things to go, but of one thing she was certain, she wanted his arms around her, his lips on hers and their love whispered between them.

Stan reached for the bottle of rum. Seconds later, they were both having a good drink. The fiery liquid seemed to burn in her throat, but Rose felt distinctly better after the third swig. The little shivers of nervousness which had been running up and down her back had stopped. Instead, Rose felt warm, contented and as free as a bird.

She turned and wound her arms round Stan's neck.

'Don't ever leave me,' her voice was low.

Stan held her close, 'I won't ever let you out of my sight, well, we've still got this war to settle. Once we've done our bit there, we'll be free to do whatever we like.'

He looked into her eyes. 'As soon as I can Rose, we'll be married. I'll never, as long as I live, sweetheart, ever leave you again.'

They consummated their love, each wanting to give the other as much assurance and joy as it was possible to give. They might survive, they might not. Whatever the outcome, at least they knew how much they loved one other.

They slept, awoke and made wild joyous love again before falling asleep in each other's arms. This time they were both awoken suddenly. What was it? They stared at each other. There were sounds, could it be voices? They scrambled as quickly as they could to tidy themselves. Stan peered from the tent and a blast of fresh air hit him. Far above he could see the heads of people, he heard their shouts and yelled back. Moments later, a ladder was being lowered and a fireman carefully climbed down it.

Having reached them, he looked around in amazement.

'Cor blimey, mate. You've had a lucky escape and no mistake.'

He checked as Rose crept out of the tent, his glance went from her to Stan.

'Cor, how many of you is down 'ere?'

'Just the two of us,' said Stan.

The fireman winked.

'Well mate, as I said before, you have been lucky!'

Rose dusted herself down, placed her cap firmly on her head and smiled.

The fireman grinned at her.

'You alright miss? How long you bin down 'ere then?'

Rose shook her head.

'No idea of time I'm afraid. My watch has stopped.'

She turned to Stan.

'Will we still be able to report for duty on time?'

'When was you due back then?' asked the fireman.

Stan spoke for both of them.

'Six o'clock sharp Monday morning, he said.

The fireman nodded.

'Right then young fella, it's just after five now, reckon you can both make it back if we shift ourselves.'

He beckoned Rose to start climbing and for Stan to follow her. Slowly the three started their ascent towards the lightening sky.

The light was dazzling and the noise confusing. Rose and Stan had to take different directions. They stood close together, not wanting to part but knowing they had to. Quickly, Stan wrote down the name of his ship, HMS Magic.

He took her in his arms.

'No choice about having to leave you, sweetheart. As you well know, orders are orders, but I'll be back. Don't you ever doubt it, Rose. I'll be back and, when I am, it's wedding bells for you and me. Where can I write to you? Quick! Give me an address.'

Rose scribbled down the new address of her friend's parents. She would be able to call and collect any letters sent to her. At least she hoped she would. Anyway, a settled address seemed the best method as she was constantly being moved about herself, thus, letters might take weeks to reach her. It would be far better to have an address where she could pick up her mail. A jeep arrived and, within seconds, Stan was being driven away. As the jeep turned the corner, they both waved, hearts aching, lips smiling.

*

It was some two months later and Rose wondered why she should be called to see her superior. Straightening her cap she gave a smart tap on the door. The voice of her boss sounded unusually gentle as he invited her in. As Rose went in, she was motioned to a chair. This was strange and as Rose showed her surprise, her superior nodded.

'I don't very often smoke, but there are times.'

She offered a slim cigarette case and Rose took one automatically. A cold feeling was beginning to creep over her. Only yesterday, she had called and picked up a treasured letter from Stan. In it, he had outlined his plans for their future and it had given her hope. Rose needed all the hope she could muster. For now, she knew beyond any doubt, that she was pregnant. Was this why she was here? Had the news been passed on already, were they going to boot her out of the service? Oh God, she couldn't have stayed on much longer anyway. She looked straight into the eyes watching her. There was no scorn, no condemnation. Rose stared.

The superior's gentle eyes closely watched her and Rose felt a gnawing fear which began to clutch at her. Such an interview was given to members of her unit when... *Oh God no, please God no.* Half rising, Rose let her cigarette fall to the floor. The words said to her seemed to come from a great distance. They seemed disjointed but one sentence beat remorselessly at her. The ship on which her beloved Stan was serving had gone down with all hands.

As the inert figure of Rose was carried out, her superior wondered why one of her best girls had to fall in love so easily and why in God's name did they have to get themselves pregnant? Oh well, it seemed this innocent girl had fallen by the wayside. Report had it that the father of her unborn child had gone down with his ship. A deep sigh escaped the woman's lips. Surely a nation could see in its heart to treasure such a child rather than brand it throughout its life as a bastard. She made a few notes after finishing her cigarette. Rose Bamber had proved a sound member of the unit, an asset, yes indeed, Rose Bamber was worthy of a helping hand in her hour of need.

The officer, known privately to her unit as Captain Flint, made enquiries and finally went to see Rose.

*

An elderly lady, living alone except for a housekeeper and gardener, was looking for a companion, provided that Rose took on the title of Mrs Bamber. The lady was called Mrs Rogan and she was quite prepared to keep her on after the baby was born. Rose was overwhelmed and wondered how she would ever be able to thank her. At first, she felt she just wanted to walk into the sea and disappear. She wiped a quick tear from her eye and believed that anyone else would have thrown her to the wolves. She looked straight at her ex-officer and said she would never forget how she had looked after her like a sister. The officer confirmed she was more than happy to take care of her.

The two women looked at each other and on an impulse Rose took the other's hand.

'Please tell me your first name. If my child is a girl, I shall call her after you.'

The officer looked at the expression of the earnest young woman. A fleeting reminder of a time best forgotten during her green and salad days was quickly brushed aside. After a moment, she suddenly smiled and relaxed. With an unaccustomed wink, she spoke softly and confirmed her name was Iris.

She threw back her head and laughed out loud.

'A right pair of flowers, aren't we?'

Rose laughed with her, but a note of something she couldn't fathom sounded in the voice of the older woman.

The officer was suddenly brisk and more like her old self.

'I'll just leave you with a few more details, then I must get back.'

As she left, she shook hands with Rose.

'Good luck. And God bless you, my dear,' she said.

Rose stared at the retreating figure. The nickname, Captain Flint was decidedly undeserved. Rose wondered if they would ever meet up again. It hardly seemed likely; someone with a career in the armed services and an unmarried mother living somewhere out in the sticks. Her new life was before her, God only knew how difficult it might be. Still, whatever happens, thought Rose, I will do my best for my baby. Somehow I'll give my child a decent life, whatever it takes. Stan's son or daughter will be loved and wanted every day of its life. Quietly she closed the door and, going into her bedroom, began sorting out her clothes. In a few days, she would travel north to Newcastle upon Tyne. She hoped reverently that she would get on with the old lady and, that as a companion, she would prove satisfactory.

Mrs Rogan, she had been informed, was a somewhat testy, but nevertheless at times, a very entertaining person. As an army wife, she had travelled extensively and now a widow in her late forties, she lived alone. Her family consisted only of a couple of nieces and for this reason she had decided to take on a companion.

How her Commanding Officer had come to hear of the job, Rose couldn't imagine. Why she should have cared about Rose was another mystery. Everyone knew that girls who allowed themselves to get pregnant without being married deserved all the scorn and unforgiving that their friends and relatives could shower upon them. That at least was the thinking of misguided generations who saw it as their duty to make the lives of such sinners as miserable as possible.

Iris had made it her business to see that at least this sinner had a light at the end of her tunnel. Rose boarded the train at King's Cross, put her case on the rack and settled back to consider her new life. When the train arrived at Newcastle upon Tyne, she would alight at platform number nine. There would be an iron bridge to cross, she would then be in the main entrance to the station. Once outside, under the portico, she would find a taxi rank. Rose furrowed her brow, surprising herself at how easily her childhood games with her father had brought back to her this information. They had never been to the North East, but two girls in her unit had come from the coastal area of Blyth. Their joyful rendering of the famous song 'The Blaydon Races' on many occasions, had left the listeners with vivid pictures of the area, and in particular, Scotswood Road. Rose wondered if she might see for herself, some of the well remembered streets or pubs so well depicted in the song. She eagerly looked forward to her first glimpse of the area which boasted such strong characters as 'Coffee Johnny', the cider sellers and the lads and lasses who had made the historic ride to the Blaydon Races. It would, of course, be their descendants who lived in the area now.

She sighed again, knowing it would just be Stan's child and hers who would follow on his tradition of living in the North East. The eventful journey to the Blaydon Races and the hilarious happenings once there, told such a tale that, once heard, it could hardly be forgotten.

Rose stirred as the journey north would soon be over and her new life as Mrs Rogan's companion would soon begin. In six months her child would be born.

'Please God,' she prayed. 'Let my child live, let it be well, help me give it a good life. Do that, dear God, and I shall give you my eternal thanks in prayer.'

The train pulled into platform nine. Rose crossed over the iron bridge, and there, in front of her, were the great pillars which held up the magnificent portico.

Walking smartly through the entrance, she hailed a taxi. A large black 'Slater' pulled up and she got in.

'Where to, miss?'

The soft northern accent came as a shock to Rose. At its sound, a picture of Stan misted before her eyes. She was going to have to get used to this. Anyway, she comforted herself, the sound of such voices would help keep Stan's memory ever fresh and even more alive. Leaning forward she offered a small card.

'Haven't a clue about the area I'm afraid, but that is the full address.'

The driver studied the card, nodded and started the engine. High Copperas Lodge - he knew the house, he knew the little hamlet of High Copperas. The villagers were a hard-working lot. The Lodge, where once the squire had lived, now belonged to a rich old woman. She had a bit of a reputation as a tartar and he wondered if his fare were a relation. It certainly sounded like she might be, with her posh voice and smart bearing. He had noticed that as soon as she came out of the station. Forces training in that one, he had thought.

'Where is Scotswood Road?' Rose suddenly asked as the taxi pulled away.

The driver waved a hand. 'Straight on miss. We'll be turning up towards the West Road.'

They were moving slowly out into the traffic. He was about to veer right when she spoke impulsively.

'Can we go that way?'

Quickly, he signalled left and turned into Scotswood Road.

'Not the quickest or the prettiest route mind but if that's what you want miss.'

They drove into a wide busy road and she wondered suddenly how often Stan might have travelled this very part. Trams, buses, cars, horses and carts, men, women and children all mingled in the busy life of Scotswood Road. The houses, flats, shops and pubs used up every inch of the tall buildings.

'Where is Armstrong's factory?'

The words of the song were coming back to Rose.

'I'll bet you've been listening to The Blaydon Races somewhere,' the driver laughed.

His voice reminded her of Stan, he waved an arm towards the left.

'Most of it runs along the river banks. Thousands work there, day-shift, night-shift, production never stops, never will till those blasted huns are beaten.'

The taxi made its way down the seemingly endless road. The pavements were packed with people going about their everyday business. Shops of all descriptions displayed their wares. It may have been war-time, things might be in short supply, but the necessities of life could be found on Scotswood Road. The hardware shops hung tin baths, buckets, brooms and all manner of such items on the walls outside. Big shops, little corner shops and huge co-op stores, all were to be seen. A spiv type, in low brimmed hat and long overcoat with wide pockets, watched the taxi as it nosed along the busy road. The pubs had beautiful stained glass windows.

'Probably made at the Lemington Glass Works, just a few miles further on,' the driver nodded.

Glancing out to her left, Rose saw a huge sign proclaimed the name Rosens & Son Ltd. She asked what it was.

'Oh that's a sewing factory, miss. Employ hundreds they do, well trained the girls are at that place".

'Sounds as if the whole area is highly industrialised.'

Her reply made him smile.

'You can say that again'.

He began to sum her up. She was certainly a stranger to the area, sounded really interested in the place, she was bright; her accent was genuine enough; she was visiting one of the best houses in the district and he might just be lucky enough to get business if it was needed. He hoped so, he was sick to death of those Yanks. A great ship full of them was anchored in the Tyne. At nights, the sailors rowed ashore and the girls fell for them hook, line and sinker. He grinned mirthlessly at his own joke.

'We are about two thirds of the way along Scotswood Road now, this part is called Benwell, miss. I'll be turning right at Atkinson Road, from there, it'll be a bit uphill, then once at the top, a sharp turn left and it's only a short run from there.'

'Oh thank you,' said Rose, glad of the geographical chat.

Her mind, trained from childhood play to remember places and distances, now soaked up the information of her new home town.

At last, the taxi slid to a halt. It had just driven through a small pleasant hamlet, turned into a wide drive and crunched lightly over pink gravel.

Rose sat for a moment, glancing out at the big house which was now her home, at least some small part of it was to be her home. A flat-let, she had been informed, was to be regarded as her own. Now she studied the house, it made a lovely picture with the late afternoon sun glinting over it. A large detached stone built Victorian town house. It stood in its own grounds looking solid and dependable. Well tended gardens ran up from the double gates on either side of the drive. They continued up the sides of the house and disappeared round the back where high trees waved their branches.

The driver got out, came round and opened the cab door. With a fast beating heart, Rose alighted. Slipping her hand into her pocket, she brought out a pound. With a smile, she glanced at the clock. The cost was less than half what she had given the friendly cabbie. He appeared to find change and she shook her head. She picked up her case, squared her shoulders and felt this was probably the last time she could be generous. He thanked her and his voice reminded her once again of Stan. Touching his cap, he got in, turned, gave her a quick smile and drove off. With an even faster beating heart, Rose walked up to the door and gave a smart knock.

Chapter III

Without a sound, the door was suddenly opened. The face which confronted Rose was plain with watery blue eyes and a halo of thin fair curls. The woman was short, looked to be in her thirties and seemed uncertain.

'Rose Bamber. I am expected.'

Rose tried not to feel irritated as the woman had looked at her up and down and was now staring at her as if she looked like someone from another planet.

The door opened wider and, in a cold and uninviting way, she was asked to go through. Rose entered the hallway, waited while the door was closed and followed the woman as she walked down a passage. At a door on the right, she knocked and entered and Rose followed. Mrs Rogan sat at a small table in the window recess and held out her hand as Rose approached her.

'Come in, my dear. How do you do? Hope your journey wasn't too bad.'

Rose took the proffered hand and shook it warmly. Whatever the lack of welcome at the door, at least her employer seemed hospitable.

'Yes thank you, my journey was very pleasant.'

The two women assessed each other. They were about the same height, probably five feet seven or so. Mrs Rogan carried more weight but her bearing was regal, she knew how to stand and move, her voice was strong and confident. She wore a smart French navy, well cut, dress with a hint of blue in her elegant hair. She reminded Rose of many of the army friends of her late mother. Her father used to laugh and call them the parade of duchesses. Rose smiled slightly at the memory and Mrs Rogan also smiled.

'Good, that's what I like to see, a cheerful smile, can't abide wishy washy crying over spilt milk. Got a problem, deal with it, that's what I say.'

She looked at the young woman in front of her. She was as smart as a carrot, spoke well and walked well. It was easy to see the army influence there and she felt in her bones that this idea was going to work out well. She walked towards the door.

'Hope you like the flat-let. I'll take you up and if there's anything which seems too ghastly to live with, well, just speak up. I prefer my antiques but, of course, you young things like furniture to be small and modern.'

Following in the wake of Mrs Rogan, Rose wondered why her employer should be bothering to take her up herself. What she didn't know was that now she had met Rose Bamber, Mrs Rogan felt drawn to the girl, for more than one reason.

The flat-let consisted of a spacious sitting room, and even larger bedroom. A sectioned off area was stripped with cane curtains across it. Mrs Rogan explained it was originally a huge linen cupboard which she thought Rose might wish to turn it into a small nursery when the time comes. Rose felt her heart lift. Surely, her employer must be the most thoughtful person on earth – fancy her even giving a thought to the unborn child. Rose turned and spoke from her heart.

'Mrs Rogan, I really am so very grateful to you for giving me the post of Companion. Being pregnant, I didn't know what I was going to do, couldn't seem to plan anything. I don't pretend to understand why you should be so kind to me, but one thing is certain; I'll never forget or let you down. Ever.'

Mrs Rogan's voice carried a slight gruffness.

'The reason I did, was as much for my benefit as yours. I need a companion who can converse with me about army life, India, the world of travelling soldiers.'

She glanced at Rose.

'I understand you were born into an army family, travelled extensively with your parents and even *joined up*, as they call it.'

Rose nodded and told her that she had joined the WRNS where she loved the life. Although her schooling was very sketchy, her late father had taught her so much about railways, timetables and destinations and although it had seemed boring to her at the time, it became useful in her work. Certainly, her superiors were always asking her to pinpoint times of arrivals etc.

'I hope you will settle in after all that excitement. Life here is very quiet you know... the village half a mile down the road, and Newcastle about five miles away. We do have a picture-house and a few pubs, but that about sums up our entertainment. Home entertainment is about the best bet now.'

She smiled at Rose.

'I, at least, won't have to go out of the house for a decent conversation,' her voice had a tinge of softness. 'Anyway, we are both in a bit of *no man's land* as it were; me an army widow, and you, well, as near as damnit, a naval widow, who cares about the might have beens? Your young man would have married you if he could have. As it is, he's given his life for his country. I see no reason why you and your child should be pilloried because of a technicality.'

Rose turned and spoke gravely.

'Yes, Mrs Rogan. My Stan would have married me. We did what we did because... well, because we both believed that we would never get out of that cellar alive. We loved each other and that was all we had left.'

A new firmness came into her tone. 'You have taken me in, offered me a life-line. I pray to God that anything I can do in return will be adequate, if only it is, I'll be glad to stay with you as long as you need me.'

Mrs Rogan looked at the young woman. Integrity and gratitude shone out of her. The violet eyes, so like those of her father, now gazed at Stella Rogan, just as his had done, more than twenty years earlier. For the life of her, she could not stifle the sigh which escaped so audibly.

*

As a young girl in Ireland, she had met and fell deeply in love with Edward Bamber. He was then a tall, shy, handsome friend of her soldier brother. The two young men had decided to spend Christmas together at the home of John Newby. His family were wealthy. The luxurious home life would be a pleasant change for Edward Bamber who, although well-educated and destined for a fine career in the army, nevertheless, had only an ordinary family as his background. In fact the family was very poor, but an uncle paid for his schooling on the understanding that he made the army his career. Since they were both destined to go out to India at Easter, John Newby, almost on a whim, asked his friend to stay with him until they sailed. Thus, it was that two weeks before Christmas when Stella Rogan met, and fell in love with, a man she was never to marry.

The Newby family had a maxim – anyone who entered into it had to bring with them as much fortune as they themselves had. They might have made their money in the early days from sweated labour and producing fine linen, but they spent a good deal of it on land where they raced horses. This being the case, anyone coming into the family had to add to the stockpile, not take from it. Thus, by dint of deceit, the young lovers were made to think that each had forgotten the other. Letters penned so desperately were cruelly confined to an all-consuming blaze.

As time went by, Edward became an Officer, he met and married the delicate daughter of an army Major. Laura Cadell had known nothing else but army life, so settled down with agreeable tolerance to the rigours of no settled home and the income of a Captain.

During their time in India, her health suffered quite considerably, thus it was that Edward was obliged to attend certain functions on his own.

Such are the coincidences in life, that one occasion found him being partnered into dinner with the wife of a Major who was in hospital. The wife turned out to be Stella Newby, now Mrs Rogan.

They had danced afterwards on a moon kissed lawn. The stars above were no brighter than those which shone in their eyes. Hearts which had secret closed off sections, opened and reached out for warmth. Love which had been denied and buried deep within them, now sprang to life and blossomed. For one brief night, they stayed together, loved together and, in the morning, cried together. Soon, their lives would take them on different paths. There was nothing they could do to change things. Edward had an infant daughter only a few weeks old, his wife was not strong. How could he leave them? He couldn't; he wasn't that kind of person.

Just before he left India for yet another posting, Stella called to say goodbye. Gazing down at the tiny child she felt resentment seep into her. The infant's great violet eyes opened and stared at her. A feeling of guilt and remorse flooded over her, she bent low and whispered.

'Sorry baby, you are not to blame for the way things turned out. Our lives take us where we must go, oh, but you do have your father's eyes. Goodbye lovely baby, love him for me, just a little.'

Her farewell to Edward was courageous but equally as sad. 'Take care of yourself, I'll never forget you, or your child.'

He took her hand, his voice dropped.

'Goodbye, my lovely wild, Irish rose. I'll always love you.'

They had then looked at each other and there was a long look of unspoken words which told of fine first love, joy of having known each other and a kind of gratitude. The sigh which escaped her lips was decidedly audible.

*

Now more than twenty years on, those same eyes looked at her with near enough the same expression. Stella Rogan felt as if she were caught in a time warp. Strange how the eyes could mean so much, perhaps they really did mirror the soul. She gave herself a mental shake. This was no time for dilly dallying, the girl had a problem, she would help her with it and she would do that because she had enough humanity in her to help anyone in trouble. Stella Rogan knew in her heart why it was that she was really helping Rose, it was because she was the daughter of Edward Bamber. With another mental shake she became businesslike.

'Breakfast will be brought up for you at nine o'clock. I shall expect you to present yourself at ten-thirty. We shall then discuss the business of the day. There will be some days when I won't need you at all, on those days please feel free to do as you wish. We shall have lunch and dinner together. I will expect you to be flexible, as of course I will be,' she said gently,

She looked steadily at Rose.

'The keys to your flat are on the sideboard. Apart from breakfast being served, no-one will ever enter without being invited.

'I've just had a thought, I'll tell Miss Briggs to leave your morning tray on the table outside the door. I have been given to understand that early mornings can be awful during a pregnancy.'

The two women looked at each other,

'As soon as possible, I'll need to register with a doctor and get booked into a hospital,' said Rose hesitantly.

Mrs Rogan nodded.

'I'll have my own man Dr Moorbath call on Monday morning. I can assure you he has a great name for the job in hand.'

Once again, her brogue had made her voice sound joyfully Irish.

'Oh thank you, you couldn't be kinder if you were my own mother,' smiled Rose.

Mrs Rogan, for the first time in her life, felt almost faint. The girl was looking at her with her father's eyes and it was almost for a second, as if he were there in front of her. She turned towards the door, continuing to talk over her shoulder.

'Bathroom right next door, kettle is already filled. Thought you might like a private cup of tea later. Oh yes, please feel free to use the telephone, it's in the hall.'

She opened the door, turned and smiled.

'I'll leave you to settle in, hope you have a good night.'

She gently closed the door and felt she needed a damn good drink. Three pink gins later, she muttered comfortingly to an old, well-loved photograph of herself and a very boyish looking Edward Bamber.

'We never let her down then, don't worry Ed. I won't let her or you down now, when she looks at me with your eyes... oh dear God, it's you looking at me again. I swear to you me darling, I'll have a care of her so I will.'

Left alone at last, Rose immediately looked for the switch where she might plug in the kettle. It was at the side of the fireplace. She quickly looked into the sideboard and drew out a tray. It held a nearly full milk jug, a full sugar basin, two cups, saucers and plates. A full glass-topped jar of digestive biscuits beside a folded napkin which held spoons and a knife. Someone had thought of everything. Setting the tray on to the marble hearth, she made the tea and settled down in a chintzy armchair.

Tomorrow, she would begin her new life as a companion. Everything she had ever heard about the job gave her the shivers. Women who were companions to army wives or widows, had always seemed to Rose to be self-effacing, shy, overworked and underappreciated. She hoped that she might never become like them.

Going to the bathroom, she quickly rinsed the cup and teapot out. In the bedroom she opened one of the dressing table drawers and was immediately transported back to childhood. Her mother used to place double layers of tissue paper in the drawers, between the layers, hundreds of rose petals would be scattered so everything from the drawers would smell fresh and feminine. There were no petals here. Still, it wasn't the time for them yet, come the late Summer and those rosebushes outside would be dropping them in heaps. She would gather them then and would lay them between the layers of tissue and she would feel closer to herself and all of the things which had made her what she was. Her upbringing had been strange, please God, this child within her, would never be left to fend on its own, never be so alone that it needed a lifeline from a stranger to help it.

Going over to the window she was about to draw the curtains when a sound caught her ear, and looking down into the back garden, she saw a tall man pushing a barrow. With slow, limping steps he followed the winding pink gravel path until he reached the shed. There he lowered the barrow and, with deliberate movement, opened the door and went inside. A moment later he had the barrow inside. He locked the door, glanced round and began walking back towards the house. As Rose watched, he suddenly looked up, for a moment their eyes held, then, with half a smile, she reached up and drew the curtains.

Ben Carter continued his way to the kitchen. Jenny would have the kettle on as she always made him a cup of tea or cocoa. Jenny was an old-fashioned lass who had been dropping a few hints lately about how well they got on together, how they both had a decent income, but what that had to do with Jenny Briggs, he couldn't fathom. Well, perhaps he *could* as he knew in his heart that Jenny would marry him at once if he asked her. He liked her well enough but, there had always been a 'but' at the end of his thoughts about Jenny. She was as plain as a pikestaff. Still, she was respectable and that went a long way with Ben Carter, but again, that 'but' was there. That companion now, there was a lass with looks, pride, dignity. He had seen her arrive and her athletic march to the front door had impressed him, but not only that, he hadn't meant to look up at the flat which he had worked so hard in. It just so happened that when he did, she smiled at him like the Mona Lisa.

Rose lay in bed thinking about all sorts of things. The world was changing. It was said that after the war, the class system would disappear. The army had a class system all of its own. The pecking order had always been very clearly defined. Anyone trying to take over was put down quickly and firmly. Those Indians who had offered their absolute loyalty and trust to the Sahibs, the Mem Sahibs and their children, were often treated like slaves; not worthy of the least consideration. Not all army families had treated their servants badly, but Rose felt a shiver go through her when she remembered some of the sad stories. Rose shook her head, the 'haves' of this life would hang on to their power over the workers till the very last. There were, of course, the unions, their strength was growing, but how long would they last? A day would surely come when someone with the sleight of mind, would be strong enough to divide and thus conquer. Then within a short time, the poor would be back on the low paid treadmill. A sigh escaped Rose and she fell into a dreamless sleep.

*

It was September and Rose and Mrs Rogan were getting along better than both had ever thought possible. Very often their wholehearted laughter could be heard as people and events were remembered. It surprised Rose, how many of her late mother's friends were known to her employer. Mrs Rogan would pour herself a pink gin, always asking Rose to have a drink as well. However, Rose kept to soft drinks as she had been told by the charming Dr Moorbath that liqueur could sometimes be harmful to an unborn child. This was enough for Rose to ensure that she took none. This child was precious. The only regret about its birth would be the fact that it was illegitimate. On this point, Rose ached inside but there was nothing she could do about it. The best she could do, as she saw it, was to have the child, love and cherish it, and hope that when it was old enough to comprehend, that an understanding of life would be sufficient for it to forgive the facts of its birth.

In the late afternoon sun, she walked in the back garden. There had been a wind earlier in the day and many rose petals lay beneath the bushes. She bent down and picked as many as she could. She was so absorbed that she didn't hear the footsteps of Ben Carter as he approached. At the unexpected sound of his voice, she quickly stood up. For a moment, the garden seemed to spin. It was only his strong arm which steadied her as she gasped.

'Oh, oh thank you so much Mr Carter, sometimes I...'

'Never you mind, you'll be alright now,' he said as he looked at her.

'Might I ask what you were after? If you'd like a few roses for your place, I'll soon pick up a bunch for you.'

Rose smiled at him.

'Oh, that is kind of you, but it was only petals I wanted.'

He looked at her in surprise, she went on to explain.

'When I was in India, my mother always used to put rose petals in the bedroom drawers. It made our things smell nice.'

He nodded. 'I see, well, if you like, I've a few muslin bags in my shed, I'll gather your petals for you, save you having to bend, like".

He suddenly looked embarrassed.

'Would you like my arm back to the house? Wouldn't do for you to be having a fall just now.'

Rose was warmed by his genuine concern and she smiled again and linked her arm in his. The pair made a slow, dignified journey towards the back door. From the kitchen, Jenny Briggs watched and her heart raged.

Chapter IV

From the very first time, when that uppity madam had handed the cabbie a pound then laughed off the change, well hadn't she seen it herself, not to mention the airs and graces afterwards. Well, hardly did a hand's turn. Oh yes, she did the flowers, always did her own flat and never asked Letty to do anything for her. Still, that only went to show that she wasn't used to servants. Jenny had no idea just how well used to servants Rose had been until she joined up. Lighting a cigarette, Jenny blew out smoke still muttering to herself. Her hopes of bringing Ben Carter round to a proposal seemed to be lessening lately.

Her sister, Joan, was the village postmistress and married to Fred Hall, who was postman. They ran one side of the Post Office shop as the required Post Office counter, with its high grille, but the other was quite a going concern as a haberdashery. Oh, they were so well organised and so damned comfortable, Jenny felt like screaming every time she was reminded of her single status. She might be housekeeper to one of the richest women in the district, but what were her prospects? What would happen to her when the old girl died – she'd be out as well as bag and baggage, then what would she do? Jenny bit her lip as her mind went back to last New Year's Eve.

There had been a dance at the village hall. Having plied Ben Carter with a number of tots at the lodge, she slipped him a hip flask of excellent old malt at the dance – the bonhomie of a new year had almost clinched it. The spiteful remark of her sister that *almost isn't quite enough, is it? What you want is an actual proposal* had gone deep with Jenny. Ben Carter had clumsily danced with her. He had clung to her arms, not so much because he didn't want to let her go, he didn't dare let her go in case he fell down. Outside they had tottered, she with her mind as clear as a bell, he, hardly knowing where he was or where he was going. Arriving at the lodge, it was a struggle but somehow she managed to get him indoors. As soon as he hit the bed, he passed out.

Taking off his jacket, she slipped his braces down over his arms. Nervously, she undid the top two buttons of his trousers, couldn't bring herself to go further, so took off his shoes. She hid them under the settee. After all, if he awoke before she did, he could hardly slip away without his shoes. She carefully pulled the eiderdown from under him, draped it round her short, dumpy body and went through to rest for a few hours on her settee. She would be up well before Ben, she would say nothing, no reproaches, but she fully expected a proposal over the breakfast table. It was the least he could do if he was ever to look her in the face again.

Alas for Jenny, just before lying down, she noticed the hip flask lying on the floor. Picking it up, she put it to her lips and swallowed a good tot. Settling herself as best she could on the settee, she smiled. A nice little sleep now and she would be bright and ready for the New Year in the morning. Tomorrow was the start of 1944 and in that year, she'd become Mrs Ben Carter and on this happy thought, she slipped into a dreamless sleep.

So well did she sleep, that she heard no sound when Ben, much more used to drink than she was, awoke with a thirst and got up to go to the kitchen. When he realised where he was, he could hardly believe it. Oh God, what had he done? He could remember nothing after leaving the village hall. Creeping towards the kitchen, he glanced into the little sitting room where he saw Jenny snoring her head off. He looked at his watch and realised it was five o'clock. He felt it would be better all round if he could get himself home. As he turned back into the bedroom, he wondered where his shoes were. He was scared in case Jenny should awake, and he found himself having to apologise so decided to slip away as quietly as possible.

It was then he remembered his wellingtons in the shed. In minutes, he was pulling them on, then, with a quick uneasy glance at the house, he walked down the drive. It was a relieved Ben Carter who finally climbed into his own bed with his last thoughts enough to make him grin. The thick flakes of snow, now falling so heavily, would soon cover his tracks to the shed. Living above the local fish and chip shop, the aroma never really left his little flat.

After a couple of hours he awoke, wretched, got up, made a pot of strong black tea, drank every drop and then went back to bed. He slept soundly and didn't awake until late afternoon.

When Jenny opened her eyes, she had to study for a moment, then she remembered. With quick movements, she dressed herself and went through to the kitchen and put the kettle on. She hummed to herself. Ben would be spark out for a bit yet. She looked at the clock and it was half past seven. She didn't need to start breakfasts for an hour yet. By that time – she hugged herself – she'd be engaged. At the thought, she could wait no longer and, going to the bedroom door, she opened it inch by inch.

For a moment, she couldn't believe her eyes. *Where was he?* She looked quickly behind the door. He was gone. Her mind began to take it in. *He was gone!* Ben Carter had slept in her bed (not that she had been in it with him). Still, he didn't know that and now, he had up and flit, just like a thief in the night. He had run out on her. Running into the sitting room, she looked under the settee. There were his shoes. Oh, God. He must have gone home in his socks. She not only felt frustrated, but deeply hurt, and she took his shoes and hurled them across her bed. They slipped down the far side and Jenny, turning to leave the room of her future nightmares, slammed the door so violently that her favourite vase fell and shattered. To add to her discomfort, some days later, Letty, the cleaner, came out from giving the bedroom a good 'do', with the offending shoes in her hand. Silently, she placed them beside the boot box for cleaning. Not a word was said about the shoes by either woman. Each, however, had her own thoughts.

When finally presented with his shoes, Ben Carter had the grace to flush up and he hung his head looking sorry.

'I must've been a damned nuisance. Sorry about getting drunk like that, it was good of you to look after me. Thanks, Jenny.'

He gave her a level start.

'I must've looked a right fool. Can't remember how, but I landed home in a dress suit and wellingtons.'

Jenny had difficulty hiding her feelings. So... he'd crept out to the shed, found his rotten old wellies and slipped home. She put on the best face she could and with a mirthless smile, she shook her head.

'I did what anyone would have done. Looked after my friend when he needed me to. Here, you'd better take your shoes.

'I'm afraid Letty found them right under the bed as you must have flung them off when I was struggling with you.'

Her words froze him. For a moment, she felt a quick rising hope. He looked uncertain and shocked. Surely he was a man of honour and that being so, he must see the position he was putting her in – the fact that one of the villagers knew about him being in her bed! Jenny looked him in the face and her heart sank. Still, she wasn't done yet. No, by God, not by a long chalk. When she spoke, her tone was matter of fact.

'Don't worry Ben, we go back a long time. If people talk about us, they're leaving someone else alone.'

His immediate reaction was one of relief. Then he felt shame. Jenny was right, they did go back a long time. As children, they had played together, as teenagers, they had been known to have the odd dance together. When her mother died, Jenny had looked after her invalid father who had been a farmhand. When, after many years her father had died, a living-in job had to be found since the family had lived in a tied cottage. Now he felt that somehow he had to make up for her care of him. He would never understand how he came to be in her bed. He levelled a glance at her, had she tried to compromise him?

Surely not, he thought

'Like I said earlier, I'm sorry for getting so drunk. You had to, well... see to me.'

He remembered the nearly unbuttoned trousers and swallowed hard.

With a rush, he ploughed on.

'How about a drink at The Skiff tonight? I hear there's to be a go-as-you-please. Could you fancy it?'

He surprised himself by asking.

Jenny drew in a quick breath. This was it – the start of their courtship. She would see to it that they both enjoyed themselves and when he brought her home, oh yes, she'd learnt her lesson, she'd have a proposal out of him before midnight. Thus it was on that occasion, Ben would ask Jenny out. At no time, however, was there any talk or sign of an understanding. Frustrated, but still nevertheless determined, Jenny accepted that it was going to be a long job. However long it took, Jenny was set on marrying Ben Carter.

The Post Office-cum-Haberdasher was very busy. A queue of people waited at the counter, while another queue stood at the shop side. A long-awaited consignment of wool had just come in and customers were sorting out their coupons. Just about everything was rationed and it took more than money to obtain goods. One also had to have the highly prized and much sought after coupons. Spivs ran a black market on every other corner and everyone seemed to have something with which to barter.

The postmistress, Joan Hall, sat behind the high grille counter. When her sister Jenny was next to be served, she gave her a knowing wink. Sliding a letter towards Jenny to see who it was addressed to, she tapped a finger on the name where 'Miss Rose Bamber' was clearly typed. It was an official letter, with a government stamp on it. Jenny gazed at the incriminating title, Miss, the letter was addressed to *Miss* Rose Bamber. Jenny felt triumphant, so that snooty butter-wouldn't-melt madam wasn't any better than she should be. It was obvious that stuck-up bitch had run away to hide her shame. It didn't matter where you lived, a bastard was a bastard and it didn't matter who you were, the disgrace was the same. Jenny grinned mirthlessly – Ben Carter would soon stop singing her praises when he heard she was nothing more than a common tart.

Joan leaned forward.

'Miss has just joined the queue,' she whispered.

'Could I ask you to see that Mrs Bamber gets this letter please – it's either that or she won't get it until tomorrow,' she asked clearly, sitting back smugly.

'Of course, I'll see to it. Can't leave important government letters lying around,' Jenny answered sweetly.

Picking up the letter and her stamps, she turned to go and, as if by accident, she glimpsed over to Rose.

'Oh, hello Mrs Bamber. I didn't know you needed anything in the village, I'd have saved you the trek,' she said in feigned surprise.

Her smile was rather like that of a fox who has just spied his supper.

'Oh, hang on. I've just been given a letter for you.'

She looked at the letter and her voice lifted as her act evolved.

'Oh, I'm not so sure though. It's addressed to Miss Rose Bamber. You are *Mrs* aren't you?'

Rose felt her face flame. So far no one had ever had cause to ask such a question. As the months had passed, she had begun to get used to the title Mrs. If only she had prepared herself for this eventuality, it had been bound to happen.

She swallowed hard and tried to look unconcerned.

'Thank you, Miss Briggs. I'm sure the letter must be for me,' she replied as she casually glanced at it.

'Looks like the phantom typist has been at work again.'

Jenny drew a deep breath. This fancy pants wasn't going to get off like that.

'Bit like a phantom lover; jumps in your bed, jumps out and is never seen again,' her voice tightened, spitefully.

'And his leavings last a lifetime.'

Her glance raked over Rose, her lips were a sneer.

Little ever happened at High Copperas and the crowd, now full of interest, watched the two women. No one had ever for a moment doubted that the well-bred, pleasant young woman at the lodge was any other than a pregnant war widow. There was plenty about, God help them. It was indeed a case of God help them as their country did very little. Now they watched avidly as the companion at the lodge was seemingly about to be 'got at' good and proper. Jenny Briggs sounded as if she might have found out some dark secret and it was all very interesting to the onlookers.

Jenny returned to the title on the letter.

'It says Miss. That is a government letter, they never make mistakes – I think you *are* Miss Bamber, not Mrs,' she gloated.

Joan Hall, in her capacity as postmistress, forgot, for the first time in her life, the rule of strict confidentiality where her work was concerned. Hadn't her sister almost got Ben Carter to the point of a proposal when this superior madam landed on the scene? Now she'd heard that he was forever carrying flowers, and even petals, into the house for *Miss Bamber*. Well, she was no more a widow than the Pope. It's time she was shown up for what she was – a tart, yes, that's what her kind were – tarts.

'If you are a war widow, how come I haven't seen your allowance book? You've been here for months and I've never seen you collect a penny. How do you account for that then?' Joan asked loudly.

Rose felt sick. The hush seemed oppressive.

Taking a deep breath, she spoke evenly.

'What my private affairs have to do with you, I cannot imagine. Why you should suddenly decide to embarrass me is also a mystery.'

She looked around – her distress was obvious – but she went on determinedly as a poster caught her eye.

'There are times when one must be circumspect. One must never forget that careless talk can cost lives.'

Her tone was even and very sad when she swept out into the cold morning air. Her words and departure caused the tide of feeling which had been stirred against her and changed to a slow resentment against the women responsible. After all, a real lady in their midst had been a pleasant change, and didn't she always have a nice way with her – always smiling – always quiet and dignified? Not at all like these two sour boots. The crowd murmured and Joan Hall gave her sister a look. Without needing to be told, Jenny slid through the rear door, praying that Joan would not be feeling as acid as she had looked earlier. It would be lunch-time in just over an hour. Perhaps then, between them, they could sort out that stuck-up madam of a companion.

She looked out of the window and what she saw sent her to open the private front door which led into the street. Having said her piece, a woman suddenly left the shop and put her arm around Rose, who was shaking. She patted her gently and comforted the distraught girl with warm northern words.

'Eeh hinny, come on pet, now you know who I am. I'm Letty, I do the rough work up at the Lodge, remember?'

Rose nodded, 'Yes, yes of course. Thank you, Letty. I don't normally let things get to me, it was just...'

'Aye, hinny. I know.'

The warm northern accent reminded Rose of Stan and tears shone in her eyes.

'Now listen, don't you let those cats in there upset you any more. Why hinny, they're only jealous of how well liked you are, aye, and I'll tell you another thing... that Jenny's had a taste of something,' nodded Letty knowingly.

'Had more than crumbs in her bed, oh aye. Knows what you had was something a damned sight better. She's just a jealous crab-apple, ignore her, she's not worth your time.'

Letty then kindly asked what she had wanted and offered to purchase them for her then offered to walk her back to the Lodge. Rose shook her head. This kind woman had just worked three hard hours scrubbing and cleaning. She had then trudged the hard road into the village and she was now offering to take her back. It wouldn't do – she had to stand up for herself. With a little mental shake, she asserted herself.

'Thank you, Letty. But I've never run away from anything in my life. I'm going back in there and I'll make that postmistress serve me, then I'll take a slow walk home.'

As they turned to go back in, Ben Carter nodded. Rose wondered if he had been in earlier as she couldn't remember seeing him and she wondered if he had been witness to her embarrassment. After a few minutes she walked in and Joan was staggered as she had her head in air. Rose asked in a steely voice for her stamps then came out to find Letty and Ben Carter waiting for her.

Chapter V

At the sight of the three, Jenny Briggs could hardly contain herself. Her voice was almost a screech as she shouted. 'Why can't you leave decent people alone? Go on, get away from here, nobody likes you and *nobody* wants you.'

Her temper was the undoing of any hopes she might ever have had. Ben Carter could hardly believe his ears. He was stunned and offered his arm to Rose who was shocked. Letty suggested he take her home after telling him of the names they had called her and the suggestion that she wasn't married.

'There, what do you think about that? Bad blood in the Briggs family – always shows somewhere – if that's one thing you can be sure of in this world, it's that bad blood will come out.'

Ben Carter had seen the look of shock and horror in her eyes at the sound of Jenny's outburst. He had heard enough to understand that doubt existed as to Rose Bamber's status. As a well-bred, educated widow, she would never have looked in his direction as a possible husband. Was it really possible that this woman, whom he had admired since his first glimpse of her, could be unmarried and pregnant? If so, the situation was a totally different kettle of fish. Such women were glad of any offer of marriage, a bastard was a bastard, and nobody had pity for either the child, or its mother. He may have walked slowly with Rose on his arm, but his mind worked cutely, with Rose as its subject. Jenny Briggs watched as the pair disappeared. She knew then that her hopes of ever catching Ben Carter as a husband were diminishing as fast as her hatred of Rose Bamber was growing. Slamming the door harder than it had ever been slammed before, she showed no change of expression when the fanlight shattered at her feet.

To Rose, the journey to the Lodge seemed endless. Without the steadying arm of Ben Carter, she felt sure that she might have fainted due to either the hurled insults or the effort of walking uphill in her pregnant state. Whatever the reason, she clung to the strong arm which steadied her until she breathlessly arrived back at the Lodge.

Within minutes of their arrival, Mrs Rogan, having witnessed the pair struggling up the drive and round to the back, hurried from her sitting room, almost ran down the passage and burst into the kitchen. Alarmed at the state of Rose, she demanded to know what had happened. Ben Carter told his mistress of the insults and humiliations by the postmistress and her sister.

Some time later, with Rose safely resting on her bed, Mrs Rogan drove her grey Ford Popular down to the village. As she screeched to a halt outside the Post Office, Joan Hall felt her heart miss a beat as she recognised her sister's employer. Like a whirlwind, Mrs Rogan flew through the door. Quick as a flash, the postmistress sent her minnion from the shop-side home to an unexpected early lunch. Almost running from her seat behind the Post Office grille, she quickly turned the shop sign to "CLOSED".

Mrs Rogan, never one to mince her words, began to speak with steely deliberation. The threat in her tone was not lost on the post mistress. As the tirade gathered momentum, the innate Irish brogue came through.

Breathing heavily, she ground out the words, 'How dare you insult Mrs Bamber, who do you think you are? And as for that snivelling sister of yours, is she here? If she is, you may just tell her to come out this minute.'

Mrs Rogan stopped for breath. She could do with a drink! She had noticed how her emphasis on Mrs Bamber, had caused the post mistress to bite her lip.

The door to the private area opened and Jenny stood there, nervously glancing from her sister to her employer. Seeing the sly looks on both faces, Mrs Rogan felt even more enraged.

Almost choking out the words, she raged, 'Mrs Bamber, I'll have you know, is from one of the best families in this land.'

She then thought of Edward Bamber who had been king of her heart for as long as she could remember. He was the father of Rose Bamber, the grandfather of the coming child. She had to say something to stop these spiteful, poisonous women's tongues wagging.

She leaned forward and spoke warningly.

'Mrs Bamber has connections who would clap you both in prison for even speaking to her out of turn, never mind slandering her. Now... do I make myself clear?' Her voice dropped.

Her words had the desired effect. The shocked looks on the faces of the two sisters would have been comical in any other situation.

'As for you, Mrs Hall, in your capacity as postmistress, you have seriously undermined your position by making public the fact that Mrs Bamber does not use a weekly allowance book.'

Staring into the now horrified eyes of Joan Hall, Mrs Rogan continued.

'Mrs Bamber is held in such high regard in government circles as a very special kind of war widow, now do you understand what I'm talking about?'

The women had no idea, although they pretended they did. A lot of secret matters went on in war-time and it seemed they had had one right in their midst and were only finding out about it now. Mrs Rogan, now quite sure that her spur of the moment excuse for Rose not having an allowance, had stopped the tongues wagging and intrigued them even more.

'Mrs Bamber has a bank account in town. Every month, an allowance is paid into it directly from army funds.'

This was a white lie. Now Mrs Rogan felt pleased that her decision to pay a monthly allowance into Rose's bank account could be explained to Rose, as her foresight in combating such gossip had now just managed to be averted.

Mrs Rogan smiled to herself. Rose had the same stubborn, but lovable, pride as her father before her. However, when she knew the whole story of how she had come to Mrs Rogan, who was more of a daughter than a mere companion, perhaps then, Rose might be able to love her, just a little.

Suddenly her vision was blurred and she felt she needed a good stiff gin and a lie down. Making for the door, she glared at the two women and felt satisfied that they had obviously believed every word. However, she felt weak, and decided to take a slow drive home, have a lie down then she would have a little chat with Rose.

'I'd like you to know, by the way, it wasn't Mrs Bamber who told me of this morning's disgraceful behaviour. It was Mr Carter. And believe me; he is as disgusted as I am at your display of wickedness. Ignorance of the situation is no excuse for slander.'

Now aghast at the turn of events, Joan Hall suddenly remembered something important. Darting behind the high grille counter, she snatched an envelope.

'Mrs Rogan, oh Mrs Rogan... This came for you only a short time ago. I... I hope it isn't bad news.'

As she took the envelope, the two women eyed each other – telegrams in war-time rarely held good news. This one was no different. Tragically, her favourite niece, Iris, had been killed in an air-raid. Seemingly she had been visiting the home of one of her girls. A direct hit had completely demolished the house. There were, of course, no survivors. It had been Iris who had brought Rose to the notice of Mrs Rogan. This was just one of those coincidences, which life has a habit of throwing up. When Iris had sent her usual letter to her aunt, outlining a problem she had with one of her girls, Mrs Rogan had read and re-read the name of the girl; Rose Bamber. That had been the name of that baby she had last seen in India all those years ago. Rose Bamber was the child of her darling Eddy. Was it fate that her niece should be writing to her about the plight of the girl? Thus, it was, that a post of a companion was thought up. It would be a stop-gap anyway. Mrs Rogan had looked forward to seeing the girl and, having met her, she took Rose to her heart and loved her. Just as it had been with her father, to know him was to love him. His daughter had the same innate goodness in her.

Now Mrs Rogan felt a searing pain go through her that seemed to dart down her arms and then tighten her throat. A few seconds of blazing light, then, gradually it began to dim.

With a long gasp, she tried to reach out to hang onto the door. She could feel herself falling. Oh God, where was Eddy when she really needed him? Seconds after whispering his name, she lay dead on the floor of the Post Office.

Joan Hall had turned away from the look on Mrs Rogan's face. As sure as eggs were eggs, a complaint was about to be put in against her. What if she did lose her job? That would be one thing, but it would also mean the loss of the house. Whoever was in charge of the Post Office always had the house to go with the job. It might even mean her husband's job as well. They would be jobless and homeless – a far cry from the successful lives they had led so far. Even Jenny would find it easier to get a job after this little lot, and it was all her fault anyway. Joan Hall ground her teeth. By God, whatever happened, her sister was shortly in for a good hard slap on the face.

Better to ask, beg even, surely Mrs Rogan might forgive this one lapse. She turned just in time to see her adversely clawing and gasping as she fell.

'Oh my God,' Joan Hall watched in horror. The old girl was having some sort of collapse.

'Ooh, Jenny. For God's sake, get some water.'

As she looked closer, the truth dawned on her. As usual, her first thought was for herself.

'Don't bother. Get an ambulance instead. Mind you, she's beyond help. There's nothing anybody can do for Mrs Rogan now – she's dead. Looking down at the inert figure, she muttered, 'No complaints now. Pity you had to kill yourself looking after that madam. Well, I don't give a damn about her or you. Now as far as I'm concerned, there won't be any complaints, no interference in our lives, the only change will be that Jenny, silly bitch, will have to find herself another job.'

So saying, she went to the door ready for when the ambulance would arrive. Jenny came and stood beside her. As Joan turned, a sharp crack rang out as she well and truly slapped the shaking face of her sister. Joan Hall had been really frightened earlier. It had all been Jenny's fault. She turned and gave her another slap. She always did a job properly!

*

As Rose drank her tea, she realised that the events of the last few days would have a dramatic effect on her life in the near future. The sudden death of Mrs Rogan had brought it home to Rose just how really fond of the old lady she had become. Strange that no mention had ever been made by Mrs Rogan of the monthly allowance paid into her bank account. Rose had always assumed that the weekly wage packet which was paid to her when Jenny and Ben Carter received theirs, had been the sum total of her wages. It hadn't occurred to her to check her bank statements. She knew she hadn't taken anything out, nor had she put money in. Thus her savings would be as they had been when she left London.

The photographs from the past had been stranger still. They had shown her own father as a very young, handsome soldier, walking or riding with an equally young, very pretty Stella Newby, as Mrs Rogan had been then. Whatever the story had been, Rose doubted if she would ever find out about it now. She sighed – Josie Malone, Mrs Rogan's niece, had made it pretty plain that she wanted the house emptied – not only the furniture, but the inmates as well. When she had offered a box of knick-knacks with old purses, photographs and odd bits of jewellery in it, Rose had been amazed to find that her father had obviously known Mrs Rogan during their green and salad days.

Josie Malone knew nothing of her aunt's younger days. Even if she had thought of Rose, she wasn't the type to put herself out by bothering with a mere companion. Josie Malone was interested in one thing and that was her inheritance. Jenny, Letty and Ben Carter, had all been given a month's wages. The house had almost been stripped and Rose knew that Josie Malone wanted to leave.

Letty, with her usual warmth had offered help.

'Just you come to us until you get sorted. You can have my big attic. His mother was up there for two years. She was as snug as a bug in a rug and you won't need to worry about the baby – it'll be as welcome as you are. Now, I know we just live in a terrace and you've been used to, well, much better. I do know that but you'd be alright. My Tom's a good sort and the kids are all in bed by seven.'

Rose had put her arms round Letty and just cried. She picked up her case and walked downstairs. Josie Malone stood in the hall. As Rose handed over her keys, she sighed. It was the beginning of November and the weather was bitterly cold but it couldn't compare with how chilled Rose felt in her heart. Josie Malone had the grace to look embarrassed and she sounded hollow as she spoke.

'Thank you, Mrs Bamber. I'm so glad you've found somewhere suitable to live and I'm sorry that I couldn't enlighten you about those photographs. You see, I haven't had much to do with that side of the family. Perhaps your father and my aunt were special friends. Anyway, it's all in the past.'

She shook her hand and wished her luck.

As the door closed behind her, Rose felt a sense of loss. Giving herself a mental shake, she was about to pick up her case when a voice spoke.

'Let me take that. Letty said you would be leaving today. Thought I'd just come up and give you a hand.'

It was Ben Carter. He came forward, picked up the case and offered her his arm. His voice had a gruff, caring note in it as he spoke.

'Letty said you'd be coming down to her place today. Thought I could carry your case.'

Rose smiled at him.

'It was kind of you to think about me. I really am grateful.'

She lifted her face and her lovely eyes - as they always had, did something to him inside. He felt proud to be just walking alongside such a lovely woman. What man wouldn't count himself very lucky indeed to be the husband of this well-spoken lady? Alright, so there was some mystery about that supposed husband of hers. So what? It had all died down now anyway. There was also that offer which his partner had made. He wanted to buy Ben's share of the smallholding which they had both worked on for years. What with the cash from that, and the money he knew she had salted away in that bank account of hers, they could even buy their own smallholding somewhere. It would have to be a distance away. He wasn't a man to have his neighbours knowing or talking about his private affairs. If only she would accept his offer, he'd do his part, be a good husband and father and, of course, in time, they'd have their own children. As far as Ben Carter was concerned, marriage to Rose would be a good thing for all concerned.

Rose received her second proposal of marriage within months of the first. However, this time, she hesitated. She might be single, pregnant and without a settled home, but she wasn't destitute. In her bank account, she had over two thousand pounds. If necessary, she could live off that until well after the child was born. Rose had only vaguely considered any further than that. She supposed that a job as a housekeeper, where a child would not be objected to, would be the answer to earning a living afterwards.

However, if she were to marry Ben Carter, his idea for a new life for them somewhere else did have its advantages. However she felt she couldn't in her wildest dreams, have ever really fancied him in that way and she didn't love him. Still, even if she did accept his proposal, her child would be born legitimate. Her child and Stan's would never suffer the indignity of being born a bastard.

Three weeks later, Rose Bamber and Ben Carter were married at the Registry Office in Saville Row, Newcastle. On the same day, they travelled to their new home across the river to Rigton, a large village a few miles from Hexham.

A few weeks later, in the January of 1945, Rose gave birth to a fine, healthy daughter. The baby was the image of her mother, with the same large violet eyes and soft curly hair. One small tiny birthmark, however, had been passed on from the Bailey family. It was a star shaped freckle on both her eyelids which was only noticeable when she closed her eyes. Rose looked in wonder at her tiny precious bundle.

Whatever she had to put up with as the wife of Ben Carter, it would all be worthwhile for the legitimising of this angel child.

How Rose wished that Stan could have seen his child. Rose thought it was strange that their love affair had been so very brief, yet his laughing face never left her memory.

Chapter VI

Rose lay holding the child close and she wondered how it had been for Stan when he died. His minesweeper, HMS Magic, had been hit by a human torpedo. What in heaven's name did that mean? Were there different kinds of such weapons? During all of her time in the service, Rose had never heard of the difference between them.

Her mind went back to the day when Stan went down with his ship. She had been told that the fleet minesweeper had carried two three-inch guns and several smaller ones. Three officers and twenty-three ratings had been killed. Her Stan had been amongst them. HMS Magic had been off the coast of Normandy on July 6th 1944 when she had been hit.

Kissing the tiny head, she murmured, 'Your real daddy was a warm, loving, laughing man. Oh, but how he would have loved you, just as I will always love you.'

Rose held the precious bundle close.

'Don't worry my love, I found another daddy for you, he's promised to give you everything and, you see angel, having a father's name is so important.'

For another hour or so, Rose gave herself the luxury of talking about Stan and remembering their all too brief affair.

Afterwards, she mentally folded away the memories. It was important to look ahead – the past was over and done with. Life with Ben wasn't always too cheerful. He was a dour, silent man and his love-making was uninspiring, but Rose was prepared to do her utmost to make the best of what she now considered to have been an all too hasty bargain. Still, so far he had kept his side of it. Rose could hold her head up, her child could never be called a bastard and as far as Rose was concerned, that was all that was important.

There were times, however, when Ben Carter did look pleased. On the day he brought his wife and baby Iris home from the hospital, a number of neighbours called to welcome the newest member of their community. Rose, with her beautiful baby on her knee, charmed them all. If the visitors thought the marriage an odd match, the local vicar's wife put them right.

'The class system is on the way out, and a good thing too. Give it a few years and you'll see the *them and us* will have disappeared.'

Another time he showed pleasure, was when, with seeming ease, Rose gave him the money he needed to buy machinery. As far as she was concerned, it was being spent on their living. Their home was a cottage, furnished as well as Rose could afford. When Ben commented somewhat harshly that the money spent on both furnishing and clothes was foolish spending, Rose put her thinking cap on.

Within the month, she secured herself a job at Durham University as an interpreter, working from home. Rose felt it was essential for people who had pride in themselves, to secure that independence.

Life in the Carter family, although poor by certain standards, nevertheless, became acceptable as a way of bringing up her child in a respectable home. When Iris was about two years old, Rose became pregnant again. Ben was delighted. He had always shown a kindly tolerance towards his step-child but, in his heart, he yearned for his own flesh and blood. It was therefore, a deep sadness to him when Rose miscarried.

Within the year, Rose fell pregnant again. Ben did all that he could to save his wife any effort. Never in his life had he put himself out so much. He carried wood, lit all fires and even accompanied her on shopping trips, insisting that she carry nothing heavy. It was a deep and bitter disappointment when she again miscarried.

This time, it seemed to Rose that he blamed her for losing their child. He began drinking and would rage at her. As the months wore on, Rose did her best to keep the peace. However, nothing seemed to please him. He became brusque and sometimes his harsh words cut her to the heart and, after one particularly heavy drinking session, he lashed out sending her spinning across the room. Unable to save herself, she crashed into the table and went down, gashing her chin on a sharp corner.

Shocked and silent, he sent for the doctor. Having examined his patient and listened to what she had to say, he pursed his lips. His patient had not only been beaten, she had been terrified. The reason for her terror was the possible loss of yet another child. When the doctor told Ben of the pregnancy, he looked shocked. It was for this reason that Doctor Holmes kept his words to a minimum to Ben Carter. He did, however, warn him that wives were not chattels but human beings – in his case, a lady beyond measure. The horror in Ben Carter's eyes showed his remorse. The doctor left with a feeling that Ben Carter would be a better husband from now on.

Going in to see his wife in their sweet scented bedroom, he fell on his knees. He took her hands and made a heartfelt plea.

'Forgive me Rose. It was the drink. But I promise you this; I'll never take another drop. From now on, I'll look after you and all of us. Let us try to have a baby that will live. Do that Rose, and I swear you'll have everything you ever wanted.'

Rose lay back and her words gave him hope.

'I'll do my best. I want this child as much as you do. I wanted them all but it wasn't to be. Still, you do your part and no one will ever know about you hitting me. The doctor won't say anything, but I want you to understand this; from now on Ben, you leave me alone. I want new twin beds at once and from now on, although I will try to be a good wife in every respect, I do not want you to ever touch me again.'

Gradually, the hope in him dimmed before it lifted. Of course, she was still in shock but would come round to normal thinking in a day or two.

He touched her hand.

'When you're up and about, we'll see to such things. You've got to rest now and no getting up until the doctor has seen you again. His orders mind, so just you stay there and I'll see to things.'

The pregnancy seemed to go quite well after that. Rose did rest much more than she had previously, and when a son was eventually born, only after a long and difficult birth, both Ben and Rose Carter were delighted that she had given him his wish.

Alas, their joy was short lived. David, as the new baby was called, suffered from Downs Syndrome. He would never be able to lead a normal life, always need someone to do everything for him. It was sad, very sad, but his parents just had to accept the will of God.

Rose brought her son home. It didn't seem possible that something as small as an extra gene could cause such havoc in the human frame. His arms, legs and trunk were perfect – it was only his sometimes staring eyes and lolling out tongue which portrayed his condition.

When visitors called, they viewed the new baby with head-shaking pity. As time went on, they became used to him in the village and many went out of their way to fuss over him. They were being kind, of course, but Rose felt her heart ache as she looked at her son.

When the vicar's wife called, she tried to comfort Rose.

'These children are special to God. They never commit sin, therefore, they never hurt him. It is indeed a wonderful thing to be able to care for one of His own angels.'

The words would have indeed been a comfort if she hadn't added, 'And you know dear, they rarely live past fourteen, so do keep that in mind.'

So saying, she left and not for one moment did she think that her words had caused an outburst of broken-hearted weeping.

Ben Carter carried his guilt secretly. He tried to help with his son, but made little headway. He tried to believe that one day there might be some hope of improvement. It was this thought that kept him going while the guilt he felt for hurting his wife, when she was carrying his child, beat at him remorselessly. Sadly though, David was so severely handicapped that learning was beyond him. His parents carried on doing their best and it almost broke their hearts in the process.

The years passed and Iris grew into a tall, lissom girl. David made only a slight improvement, learning to recognise his loved ones and showing pleasure by kicking and banging. At fifteen, Iris left school and enrolled at Skerry's College in Newcastle. Having spent a determined year studying, she passed her exams and obtained proficiency certificates in typing, shorthand and accounts. As well as the office skills, she also studied English and enjoyed French and Spanish at home with her mother. It never ceased to amaze her, just how well her mother spoke foreign languages.

Now that she was ready for the working world, Iris began watching the 'situations vacant' columns. One day she saw just what she was looking for and without further ado, sent off a letter of application. Within the week, she received a reply with a time and date for an interview.

*

Stan Bailey was amazed that he was still alive. He lay in a hospital bed trying to think clearly. His ship had been torpedoed. There had been survivors but none of his mates were among them. Like many others in war-time, he had been inadvertently listed among the missing. That must have been a hell of a shock for those at home. Still, they would now know that he was still alive and kicking – well, not really kicking. He looked at his legs.

'You'll mend in time. After that, it's civvy street for you – your bit has been done – you're one of the lucky ones, going home in one piece,' the doctor had quite cheerfully told him.

Stan had written to the address which Rose had given him in the hope that it would reach her. The reply he received just about broke his heart. The house had suffered a direct hit in an air raid. Not only had the family perished, but also a visiting WREN. Dear God, Rose must have been there, looking for her mail. Stan then went into a kind of no-man's land. It was because he'd lost his will to live that his recovery took so long. He returned home to find his parents ailing and the business had been sold to an uncle. His father wept as he told Stan how he had just lost heart in everything when he was informed that his son was dead. He had let the printing works go for a pittance and hadn't really cared about anything except being there for his wife for as long as he could.

Within weeks, both parents were dead. It was a pretty rotten world to come back to and Stan, thoroughly fed up with everything, took up his uncle's offer and returned to work in the printing shop. Some of the old workforce welcomed him back. They had a great deal of respect for young Mr Bailey, just as they had had for his father. They thought the sell-out was rotten for the lad. Still, he had been presumed dead, so, all in all, he was very lucky.

When Cara Doig, his uncle's adopted daughter, came to work in the office, she made a dead set at Stan. Her father saw the advantage of a son-in-law who knew the business and encouraged the match. Thus it was that Stan found himself married to the spoilt, pretty madam. Every chance she had, she pushed it down his throat, the fact that while he laboured in the business, she owned it and she was his boss – he would, therefore, do her bidding. Stan was at a loss to understand why, what seemed such a good idea only a year ago, was now a total disaster. His marriage was a failure. Well, in his heart, he knew that Rose still held a special place – perhaps it wasn't all Cara's fault. Things, however, did improve. It was the birth of their son, Eric, which brought them closer. At least they were united in that they both loved the boy and, for his sake, Stan put up with Cara's never-ending jealousy and nagging.

The years passed and Eric grew into a tall, pleasant young man. Having enjoyed holidays abroad, he decided to take a home study course in French and Spanish.

Miss Pierce, who had joined the firm as a young woman, now ran the office. Cara Bailey had long since given up coming in on a regular basis. She did, however, usually after one of her expensive shopping trips to town, put in an appearance. On these occasions, she would whirl into every section of the works and never missed a chance to let the workers know that she held the reigns of power. In many cases, it was only the long held respect that the workforce felt for their manager which stopped them telling her what they thought.

When Alma, the young trainee office worker gave in her notice, Miss Pierce was taken aback as she seemed so settled. Alma, however, felt she had no future with her job which she wasn't enjoying anyway and announced she was going to Butlins to be a Redcoat!

Miss Pierce went away to think things over. The next office junior would already have her typing and shorthand. It wasn't any use wasting time on girls who changed course midstream. Miss Pierce rang the *Evening Chronicle* and placed an advertisement and within days she had a dozen or so replies. She carefully picked out a number for interview and one of them was Iris Carter.

Stan was feeling under the weather. For weeks now, he'd been sleeping badly. It was always the same in April. Today was the anniversary of his meeting with Rose all those years ago. Before going into work, he'd take a walk around the square. It was funny how he'd never been able to put Rose out of his mind and funnier still, that other faces from the past had faded, but not hers, and the memory of her smile was as fresh as if he had seen it only yesterday.

He sat down on a bench. All around him, the busy square was preparing for the business of the day and soon animals, cars, people and stalls would take up every inch of space. Tuesday was market day in Hexham and people made a day of it from miles around.

Above him, the abbey proclaimed its majesty. The pace of the day was quickening. From one end of the little town, the train arrived, bringing in visitors. At the top end, people streamed out from mass at St Mary's Catholic Church. From the direction of the station, a tall young girl walked sedately towards the square and, unlike everyone else, her pace was relaxed. Her bearing was straight and erect as she made for a bench. She surveyed the scene and sat down. Stan watched the girl and as she suddenly turned towards him, he almost felt his heart stop.

God Almighty – was he imagining this? Was this April day so special in his memory, that it was causing him to see a face from the past? A face, so loved and longed for, that he would gladly give the rest of his life for just a moment of its nearness. He watched the girl in a trance. Long, curly, black hair, framed an oval face and... her eyes! Dear God! In all his life, he had only once seen eyes like them – his darling Rose had looked at him with eyes just like hers. The awful feeling of earlier had passed and now he felt as if he were in a time warp. He was seeing people he knew were dead.

Chapter VII

He gave himself a mental shake. He was being foolish and had allowed his sorrow of the day to run away with him. He felt it was far better to go to work as he had to interview a number of young ladies for the office job. Miss Pierce would have a good strong cup of rum tea for him as soon as he walked through the door.

Heaving a sigh, he rose and headed for the little printing works. He might be a third generation managing the place, but his wife held the purse strings.

As Miss Pierce handed him the steaming cup of strong tea with a dash of rum in it, she announced that the three girls were waiting in the lobby to be interviewed and he should press the buzzer when he was ready to see the first one.

Miss Pierce slipped out of the inner office and spoke through the hatch door to the three eager looking teenage girls.

'When the buzzer sounds, please come through, in turn,' she said.

The girls nodded and Miss Pierce closed the hatch. A minute later, the buzzer sounded and the first girl came through the large door. The hatch was already open so that Miss Pierce could keep an eye on the remaining girls. These two were gigglers – she wasn't going to have any of that kind of noise interrupting an interview. She quickly took Iris across her office to the inner sanctum and giving a light tap, she opened the door and announced that Miss Iris Carter was here to see him.

As the door closed and Iris advanced towards the desk, Stan Bailey thought he would pass out. Dear God in heaven, he was seeing the same vision for the second time in one morning. He tried to assert himself.

'Do you think you would like to work in an office?' he asked.

What the hell was the matter with him? Of course, the girl wanted to work in an office – that was what she was here for, to be interviewed for an office job. He decided to try again. Before he could say anything, she answered his question.

'Oh yes, I like order, and running an office is what I wish to train for.'

If her looks shocked Stan, the sound of her voice almost sent him reeling.

Dear God, who was she?

This girl who not only looked like his lost darling, had her voice too! Oh, it wasn't the same cultured tone, but by God – that lilt – he'd know it anywhere.

How he got through the interview, Stan never knew. All that he could remember was telling the girl that she could start the following Monday.

As Miss Pierce saw Iris leaving, she made for the inner office. At the sight of Stan looking quite ill, she closed the door, went to the little cupboard and poured him a tot of rum.

'I'll tell the girls to come back another day. You, Mr Bailey, should be home and in your bed.'

Stan drank the fiery liquid and gave her a smile.

'Sit down, Miss Pierce. I've had a bit of a morning one way and another. Still, I did manage one interview and I think Miss Carter will do well with us. I've told her she can start. Sorry about not discussing it with you first, but, well, if you've already put her on a shortlist yourself, you must have thought her suitable.'

Miss Pierce loved it when her boss talked to her in this friendly way. He didn't deserve that bitchy wife of his and Miss Pierce couldn't understand how he put up with the treatment she gave him for all these years. However, she was glad he had chosen Miss Carter as she herself had thought the girl was the best of the three.

Both turned when they heard a light tap on the door.

'Come in,' he called. Stan's voice sounded more like his than it had all morning. The door opened and there, framed in it, was Iris Carter.

'I'm so sorry,' she hesitated. 'When I got outside, I felt in my pocket for my return train ticket, I can't find it and I wondered if I'd dropped it in here.'

Miss Pierce swooped down and picked up the missing ticket. It had been hidden under the extra chair. With a delighted smile, the girl bent to take it from the outstretched hand. Watching her, Stan suddenly gave a gasp. She had lowered her eyelids to look down at Miss Pierce and it was then that Stan saw for the first time in years – the family trait of twin gold freckles on the centre of each eyelid!

Stan managed to hide his shock with a grunting cough. As Iris took the ticket, she smiled.

'Thank you very much, Miss Pierce. I'd have had to pay again if you hadn't found it.'

She sailed through the door and as it closed, Miss Pierce glanced at her boss. His face was ashen and he looked as if he were about to collapse. As she had often done when he was a younger man, she decided to mother him.

'Now don't take this the wrong way, Mr Bailey, but you haven't looked at all well since you came in this morning. Why don't I make you another cup of tea and then call it a day. That interview has taken up a lot less time than we had organised for. The rest of the business is straight forward. Take my advice, Mr Bailey, have yourself a good walk round the park, it'll do you a lot more good than sitting in an office on a lovely day like this.'

Stan smiled at the woman who was his secretary, and had indeed been his father's in the old days. Both men had trusted her completely and she revelled in it. She had worked from girlhood in the firm and, the fact that her bosses treated her with caring civility and trusted in her work so implicitly, only served to promote her genuine care for her employers.

Miss Pierce was an institution at Bailey's, and the only time she had ever been unhappy there, had been during the years when it had changed management.

'Take my advice, Mr Bailey. At least take a couple of hours off. All work and no play you know...'

She smiled gently as she she left the office.

Stan thought about his office staff. Miss Pierce, of course, kept everyone on their toes. She was always fair but, at the same time, demanding of the staff under her guidance. Tom Cooper, the tall gangly salesman went out and about drumming up business, then there was the office junior. Stan closed his eyes at the thought of this new member of his workforce who had knocked him for six with her face, form and even her voice. Then to cap it all, those two star shaped freckles on her eyelids – *who was she*? Could it be possible that she was a far flung member of his family? Surely not, he would have known about other branches of his own kin. No, there had to be another answer.

It was then that Stan thought about his uncle. He had always been one for the ladies – married twice and with only an adopted daughter to show for it. Perhaps he'd had an affair. Still, even if he had had an affair, the chances of him fathering a child seemed a bit bleak, Stan dismissed the unworthy thought as the old man was dead anyway. No, it was up to him to find out about the girl – he couldn't bear to wait any longer.

It was a determined but nervous Stan who drove his sleek Austin Mayflower out towards the village of Rigton. He came upon the twisty lane quite unexpectedly. Stopping nearby, he glanced over the hedge, got out and hailed the worker in the field.

'Excuse me.' He stopped at the sullen grim expression on the face of the man.

He thought swiftly, 'Can you tell me if there's a garage anywhere nearby? Afraid I'm running out of petrol.'

The man jerked his head.

'Fifty yards down the road,' he replied and turned back to his work.

Ben Carter wasn't interested in strangers who didn't want to buy his produce. Stan suddenly understood. Perhaps the man might be more forthcoming if he bought something.

He put friendly askance into his voice.

'What chance of buying any of these greens mate? Best I've seen in a long while.'

Ben Carter straightened up, his voice was curt.

'My wife is up at the cottage, she'll get what you want.'
He turned back to his work. That was more like it –

perhaps Rose had been right about putting a sign up – he'd see to it tomorrow. It had better be worthwhile as he didn't like being made to look a fool.

Rose carried the watering can to her tubs of flowers. Tipping it slightly, she gently moistened the dry earthy bed. Glancing towards the big field, she saw Ben working with hunched shoulders. She hoped he wasn't going to come in and glower all evening.

A movement in the lane caught her eye. She wasn't expecting anyone but hoped it might be a customer. With a hand raised to shield her eyes from the April sun, she watched the figure approach. As she did so, something about the way the man walked struck her.

He was sea trained – she'd bet on it – that slight roll as he walked.

Oh dear God!

She suddenly started to shake.

It couldn't be... it certainly looked like... Oh, but that was *impossible*. The man walking towards her was like a ghost from the past. This person, whoever he was, he couldn't be Stan. Darling Stan had been dead these long years. As he neared, she almost collapsed. It WAS Stan! He was looking at her and holding out his arms.

Stan saw the woman turn and look in his direction. As he did so, he caught his breath. It had been a day of shocks and surprises. He had met up with a young girl who had instantly reminded him of the only woman he had ever really loved, not only that, but he had seen the birth marks on the girl which had driven him to find out about her parentage. Was he imagining that he was actually face to face with...

His heart leapt, his throat suddenly went very dry, his voice held cracked disbelief as he spoke her name.

'Rose,' he went towards her, arms outstretched. Her face was suddenly heaven-lit with happiness.

'Stan!' they embraced and, for the first time since they had parted, both knew deep-felt happiness.

Hand in hand, they walked round to the rear of the cottage. There seated beneath the scented shade of two great lilac trees, they talked, pouring out the stories of their lives. As the tales unfolded, each felt an aching sadness for the unhappiness of the other. Each had loved and each had lost. Both had settled for what life had offered, both had accepted love from others of the second best kind, neither had found life easy.

Suddenly Rose stiffened and a look of alarm crossed her face.

'We can't talk any more, you'll have to go as I've got to see to David.'

There were loud noises from the open barn where David was trying to manoeuvre his wheelchair. In a second, Stan rushed across and pushed David into the shade beside them where they faced each other over the top of the wheelchair. Stan winced inside at the deep pain in the violet eyes.

Dear God, how Rose had suffered. Not only by thinking he was dead, but because of that and finding herself pregnant, which incidentally had been his fault, she'd had to accept the first offer of marriage, which would give their child a name. He closed his eyes but her urgent voice brought him back to reality.

'Please Stan, you must go now. Ben will be wondering why you've stopped so long already.'

She reached for a bag of vegetables and handed them to him.

'It's been wonderful seeing you again, just to know that you still share the world with me will give me heart.'

Her voice dropped but its timbre carried the pathos of lost love.

'Our lives may be very different to what we planned. Still, the thought that you are somewhere, perhaps thinking of me, just as I'll be thinking of you. That, my darling, will help me to carry on".

His reply was instant and the words made her heart sing.

'Forget that, quite suddenly, after all these years, I've found you. Come what may, lovely girl, I don't intend to walk away from such a wonderful discovery. Tell me it's the same for you, and that you at least want to meet and talk. Rose, my darling, at least say yes to that.'

As she nodded, he let out a sigh of relief. Again, their eyes met and once more, they were in each other's arms. The sorrow of years was lost as the sheer joy of being together enfolded them. Against his shoulder her voice was a hoarse whisper, but Stan heard the words, 'Tomorrow, I'll meet you in town, every last Wednesday, I go into Newcastle to pay bills and do a bit of shopping... I'll do that as usual and then I'll meet you about two o'clock in St Thomas' Square. Will that be alright for you?'

'Will that be alright? My God Rose, if you knew just how alright that sounds to me...'

His look told her everything she wanted to know. Now she begged him to go quickly. He caught the anxiety in her voice and, turning away, began to walk down the twisting lane. At the last turn, he glanced over the hedge, Ben Carter was watching him. Stan decided to be pleasant. He held up the large bag of vegetables.

'Thanks, mate. You should have a stall in the market, nothing up there to match your stuff. So long.'

A curt nod was all the reply Stan received. Still, he reasoned, the miserable dog had no cause for suspicion; after all, Ben Carter had sent him up to the cottage himself. Stan hoped, fervently, that nothing would happen to stop Rose meeting him the following day.

Watching Stan as he walked away, the reality of what was happening in their lives began to seep in. Iris would be living at home with the man she always called Dad. Ben had never wanted her told that she wasn't his own daughter. From Monday to Friday all day, she would be working in close contact with the man who was her natural father. How could she be kept from finding out the truth and if she did find out, how would that affect her? Oh dear, sometimes life was more than just a little complicated.

Supposing she did meet Stan as arranged, what might it all lead to? Mechanically, Rose set about pushing the wheelchair into the house. Although now a young teenager, David still needed to have everything done for him. She found him heavy to deal with on her own. Rose wanted time to think. Ben would have come at once, but Rose decided there were times when even a silent man would stop her train of thought.

Wednesday dawned with an early mist. As the day progressed, the sky lightened and a warming sun blessed the earth. Although living nearer to Hexham than Newcastle, Rose had rarely visited the historic town. The main reason had been that it might just have been possible for her to pass a member of Stan's family and never have known it. Somehow, that thought had hurt, although, business and shopping trips were usually made in Newcastle city centre. She wondered if she had visited Hexham years ago, she might have met up with Stan and wondered what would have happened if she had? If they had met before David was born, would they have...? She stopped herself. What was she thinking about? It didn't matter now anyway as her son would always come first. He would need her all his days and she would never be the one to let him down.

Her mind now went to the situation Stan had returned to. His parents frail and very soon to die, the family business sold out for a song to an uncle with an eye on the main chance. An uncle who had strung along his nephew, with promises of the business going back to him when he married his stepdaughter. Poor Stan; what a return to civvy street he'd had. Like many other servicemen, he had returned to find that those he had fought for had been stabbing him in the back. Why the Government had allowed such a state of affairs, Rose couldn't understand. Still, as well she knew, it happened all too often.

Rose sighed. All their suffering had been the result of Stan being wrongly listed as dead. Many of his fellow crewmen had died but there had been some survivors. He had been found in a hospital, nursed back to health and sent home. Rose sighed at the thought of her and Stan being married to different partners, who each had a responsibility towards their families. They were made of the stuff that could never forget that. To both of them, honour and integrity meant a great deal. Anyway, what could they do about mistakes in the past now? Cara, his wife, sounded a bit unstable but they had a son whom they both loved. Rose was glad of this as it meant that Stan loved, and was loved.

Apart from her children, Rose had only ever loved her parents and Stan. She had adored Iris from birth – there was a bond between mother and daughter which had always been very special. As for David, poor darling, he would never improve. The doctors had warned her that one day, he would go into one of his fits and never come out of it. His heart, which was overburdened from birth, would simply give up beating. Rose then vowed that she would give her son all the love, care and attention he required. The love Rose bore for her son was indeed every bit as natural as that for her beautiful, charming daughter.

Rose made her way from the train at Newcastle through the elegant portico into one of the finest streets of the city. Her mind went back to the first time she had done this seventeen years ago, seeming like a lifetime ago now. Just as she had done before, she wondered nervously, just what fate had in store for her. She had thought Stan was dead then, but now she knew he was alive. The joy and wonder at the discovery was still with her. Was that why she'd hardly slept all night? She had barely been able to eat anything at breakfast. She caught her breath. This strange wildness was beating at her very heart and soon she would be meeting Stan. She had loved his ghost all these years, treasuring every little memory of him, but all that was very different to suddenly finding him alive, discovering that her feelings, if anything, had intensified. What would be the outcome? Stan had made it quite plain how he felt. Neither had changed – their love for each other had never diminished – it wouldn't die because it *couldn't* die. Again, she then agonised what would the outcome be of the two of them meeting? As she completed her last errand, Rose turned towards St Thomas' Church. Somewhere in the grounds, he would be waiting for her. Her heart began to thump, her throat felt dry. At last she reached the church grounds and began walking around the narrow pathways.

Stan was waiting in a fever of anticipation. He sat on one of the many benches watching the main entrance to the church. All around them, there were adults with children, students with books, and pigeons with hopes of scraps.

To the casual observer, the meeting between Rose and Stan was quite ordinary, but to the pair themselves, it was as if the world really did stand still.

Chapter VIII

As Stan turned his head, their eyes met. He rose eagerly to meet her. She walked towards him – it was like a dream come true. How many times in her imagination had she thought of such a meeting? How many times had she ended up weeping at the sheer hopelessness of wishing it were possible? Now it was happening, every fibre of her being, gloried in the rich joy of knowing he was alive. He loved her and most of all he was the one man she would love until her last breath.

He took her hand for a brief second, squeezed it gently and casually fell into step beside her. They strolled along the little pathways and then turned out into the busy streets of the city centre. They had only gone a few yards when Rose suddenly stopped in her tracks. Her voice sounded urgent as she whispered to Stan to walk ahead. She snatched her arm away from his and fell a few steps behind. A woman passed Stan and he heard her greet Rose. The pair spoke only briefly and after a minute, Rose caught up with him.

Her voice had a catch in it.

'Worry? What else could I do?'

'Nothing,' he replied. His tone was flat. The joy of the day had been spoiled and it had been brought home to them both very clearly just how easily they could start tongues wagging.

Stan made up his mind.

'Let's go to the pictures. At least in there we can sit together without the world staring at us.'

Rose shook her head.

'On a Wednesday, some of the picture halls give concessions to pensioners. I know for a fact that half the old folks in the village will be in the town pictures today.'

Stan groaned and looked at her with a grin.

'Tell you what, let's just stroll as if we were strangers,' he winked. 'Who knows, we might just accidentally bump into each other!'

They walked off smiling. As they passed shop windows, they would glance in, catch sight of each other in the glass and laugh.

Suddenly, once again Rose sounded scared.

'Oh Stan, I know that couple coming towards us, they haven't seen me yet, but...'

Whatever she had been going to say was cut off in mid sentence. With a firm hold on her arm, Stan was urging her into a wide doorway. He quickly paid some coins at a pay desk and pushed her through a pair of wide swing doors.

Rose was shocked when she realised they were in a dance hall. Stan nudged her towards a small settee and, thankfully, Rose almost collapsed into it. Her voice was breathless as she questioned where they were. She wasn't aware that tea dancing went on anywhere outside of London. Stan informed her that it was the Oxford Galleries and that it was the best dance hall in the North East of England. Three afternoons each week they had tea dances and because Wednesday is a half day for most of the shops in town, it just happened to be a tea dance day.

He smiled at her.

'We've found a bit of luck at last. Go on, take your bags downstairs and then let's enjoy a few dances. What do you say?'

The last time Rose had been anywhere like this seemed a lifetime away. Since her marriage, the only outings she had enjoyed were trips to the local picture hall in the village.

Since Iris had been old enough to take to the first house pictures as a special treat on a Friday night, this, together with the Rediffusion radio, had been the only relaxation that Rose had known.

She followed the direction of the illuminated arrow pointing to the Powder Room. Having tidied herself up and glanced ruefully at the plain grey skirt and rather old-fashioned blue blouse she, nevertheless, felt a thrill as the sound of the band tuning up for the next number caught her ear.

'Haven't seen you here before,' the voice in her ear sounded friendly. 'First time?'

Rose looked around anxiously but she needn't have worried. The woman standing beside her was about her own age, smart, pretty and a total stranger.

'Yes, it is.' Rose knew she sounded breathless.

The stranger laughed.

'Don't look so worried. Most of us at these tea dances are walking on forbidden ground. Well, dancing if you like. My old man would have a fit if he knew where I was at this minute. Still, we've got to keep sane somehow and what harm can a few dances do?'

She smiled and shrugged.

'Anyway, if my old man doesn't like dancing, why should I have to take the pledge against it?'

Rose smiled. She felt at one with the friendly stranger.

'I know the feeling,' she softly murmured and the other winked.

'My name's Babs, by the way.'

'I'm Rose.'

The two touched each other lightly with the palm of their hands.

'Let's go up together as it's much nicer to appear on the floor with someone.'

Babs raised her eyes towards heaven and giggled. As they went upstairs, the band began to play a lilting waltz.

For some reason, Rose felt at ease. The atmosphere of friendliness and pleasure was beginning to seep into her. All around her, people were chatting and smiling. The music was so good that it seemed everything was conspiring to make her feel one of the revellers. At that moment, Stan appeared at her side. He took her hand, looked into her eyes and as if by magic, they were dancing in a thrilling close hold.

As they danced, he whispered wonderful things in her ear, held her body close to his until she felt his heart beat. Suddenly, the lights dimmed and a great coloured orb began to swing from the ceiling. As it turned, long slivers of coloured light drifted across the dancers. It was as if they were in a wonderland of pleasure where only their own world existed – a world where she and Stan might dance for the rest of their lives.

The next two hours flew by and Rose was suddenly shocked to find how late it was. She would have been expected back ages ago. She rushed downstairs, almost knocking over her new found friend.

'Steady on! Just like mine, I bet your old man will be sitting at home like a cat on a hot tin roof. Am I right?'

Rose laughed but her concern was not lost on the other.

'Well, I've got to get back. Perhaps I'll see you next week. Bye then.'

Babs watched as Rose ran up the stairs.

'Good luck. We're all the same... caught like rats in traps. Still, thank God for this place.'

Stan was waiting for Rose and it only seemed minutes had passed before she was running up the twisty lane.

Her mind was in turmoil. Stan had begged her to try and make it next Wednesday. What excuse could she possibly make? Ben was used to her monthly trips to town. Of course, they were necessary. What on earth could she use as a reason for going next week and every week after that?

Rose was amazed at her sudden capacity for telling lies. When a look of relief had shown on Ben's face at her arrival, an instant excuse had jumped off her tongue.

'Sorry I'm a bit later than usual, hope you weren't too worried. I met an old friend from the WRENS who's married and now living up North. We've agreed to meet every Wednesday afternoon for tea. Would you mind?'

Ben Carter levelled a look at his wife. He had been mad to worry about her having an accident as she always could look out for herself – why ever had he worried? She had been meeting up with her posh friends, even arranging to meet them again. He hoped she wasn't going to meet them here as he didn't want to be made to feel out of place in his own home. He grunted. His voice was harsh as he spoke.

'Do what you like, just so long as you don't bring your posh friends back here,' he said as he left the room.

A sudden rage engulfed Rose. What an ill-mannered, boorish roughneck he was. For the second time in her married life, Rose retaliated. Her words caused him to stand stock still for a moment. The absolute fury in her voice made him blink. As the pent up anger of years poured out, she ended with the words which sent him stamping out of the house.

'Bring my friends here to meet you? I wouldn't dream of it. I wouldn't want any friend of mine to meet you. You are an unbending, hard-hearted brute of a man, old before your time and trying to put us all in an early grave.'

Returning to the house later, Ben was astonished when Rose spoke to him with an edge still in her voice. He was used to her compliance to his moods and used to her pandering to him, except, of course, where sex was concerned. He still shared her room but not her bed. Since the birth of David, first his cot then his bed with its raised sides, stood between their single beds. He had only once tried to make her do his bidding. Seemingly, however, she could not bring herself to accept him. He set himself to forget that part of his life. After all, what had it brought him anyway – nothing else but a disappointed wife and a mongol son. He loved Iris, but she wasn't his child... his by name but not nature. A man could only give so much of his mind to such a child. Still, she was a source of pride; she was bright, clever and pretty. Everyone thought of her as his child. At least he had benefitted that from the marriage.

The times spent at the tea dances were wonderful. To Rose, they made up for the lost years and the humdrum existence she lived. Every week it was like falling in love all over again. The weeks went by on wings and Rose had her hair cut in a modern style. She bought make-up, new clothes and took on an air of glamour she'd long forgotten. Iris settled in at Bailey's and Rose could barely suppress a smile as her daughter enthused over Miss Pierce and the manager. She informed her family that Mr Bailey had such charming manners and was always so polite to everyone and that working for him was a real pleasure.

It had to happen; two people loving each other as they did couldn't expect their feelings to call a halt. Nature is such that she goes ever forward, ever pushing to involve and keep her hold on life.

The excitement of dancing with Stan in an atmosphere of pleasure, of talking pleasantly with other women, who, like herself, were seeking a few stolen hours away from their humdrum lives – all these things heightened her feelings and it was when dancing the tango when Stan whispered he loved her and she confirmed that she would always belong to him.

Stan looked at her as they swung in perfect unison to the throbbing music. His voice was husky.

'What did you say? Tell me it's true, tell me I didn't just imagine it. You did say...'

Rose whispered excitedly, 'Of course I feel the same, I love you, want you, Stan darling. I can't wait to be in your arms as your woman, as that's always been in my dreams.'

As the dance ended in an exciting spin, the pair swung round and round and looked at each other as if hypnotised. As the floor cleared they hardly noticed anything around them except Stan was holding her hands and gazing at her.

He marvelled at the change in her since their meeting at the cottage. She had only been a shadow of her former self then. The change in her now was dramatic; smart hair, good cosmetics, elegant clothes and there was, of course, the added bonus of that inner glow which shows so clearly when someone knows they are loved.

As they realised the floor had emptied, Rose gave a little sigh.

'Time to go. Still, it's been marvellous; I've really enjoyed dancing today.'

She looked at him and her expression made his pulse jump. He put his arm around her and whispered.

'Next time we meet, darling, let's make it really special. I'll make whatever arrangements I can to suit. One thing I will promise, darling... there'll be nothing sleazy, nothing to make you feel, well, you know what I mean.'

Yes, Rose knew exactly what he meant. Hadn't his every thought been for her feelings? Didn't he always put her first in everything they did? Never once had Stan kept her waiting, never once had he tried to make her stay just a little longer. His love for her was of the giving kind, exactly as was her love for him.

'Yes, darling. I know what you mean and thank you. I'll leave the arrangements to you. I wouldn't have a clue anyway. Just one thing Stan,' her eyes had a sad look for an instant. 'I'll have to be back at the usual time, you know how things are.'

Stan certainly knew as he hated the deceptions which they were forced to carry out. He could accept it for himself but he knew, with Rose, that it went against her nature to lie and cheat. His arm tightened around her shoulders. They glanced at each other and Stan was glad to see the fleeting sadness replaced by her radiant smile.

The band was tuning up for a waltz when they happily agreed to have another dance. He swept her to him and said huskily, 'Then, my darling, we'll go as we have plans to make. Can't start too soon for me. Next Wednesday will be for us, nothing and no-one will be allowed to spoil it, I'll see to that. Trust me, my darling, trust me.'

As the music played and the song 'Strangers in the Night' was sung hauntingly, Rose laid her head on Stan's shoulder. Of course, she could trust him. He would see to everything and, this time next week – she gave a little shiver of pleasure which he felt, then tightened his hold. They looked at each other and simultaneously whispered 'I love you.' The band played on and love, it seemed, was everywhere.

*

The days passed with the Summer now at its height. Ben Carter was a perfectionist where his produce was concerned. If his fruit, vegetables and flowers were to be the topic of debate between housewives and judges, well then, nothing but first class, was good enough for him. He put his every effort into producing the best. It was, therefore, little wonder that his name became a byword in the local shops and garden produce shows.

Since the notice had been erected on the main road, many cars, cyclists, passers by, and even buses, stopped to buy from the laden, trestle tables at the top of the lane. Rose always dealt with the customers and the cash was banked every last Wednesday. Now of course, she was going to town every week, she was also spending more on herself than she ever had in her life. At first, she had felt guilty about this but now she accepted that she had as much right to spend this money. After all, she worked hard in the cottage and at the tables. Caring for David was a hard enough job even on his good days. Now older and much heavier, Rose often felt exhausted before lunch-time on his bad days.

Wednesdays, however, were her easy days. On that day, Ben would work all morning in the field. Rose would make an early lunch for them all then Ben would take his son outside. Rose would then clear up, prepare a high tea and leave it all ready. After a quick bath and a change into something smart, off she would go into town.

Having taken his son into the yard, in the good weather, Ben would make sure that he could see, and be seen by, David. He would then sweep and swill the yard and the paths round the cottage, clean the outsides of the windows and generally make the exterior of the cottage tidy and as attractive as possible. He might be slow in his movements but Ben Carter was not a lazy man. Now he watched as Rose walked down the twisty lane. These days she was as smart as a carrot and he supposed that posh friend of hers was to blame for all the unnecessary effort she put into dolling herself up every time she went to town.

Having reached the main road and glanced around, Rose saw Stan parked just a little way back beneath the highest section of the hedge. She quickly walked towards him and got in. At once, he set off, but this week, however, not in the direction of Newcastle, but towards Hexham.

'Everything alright, darling?'

She nodded, not trusting herself to speak. All week she had been in a fever of nervous anticipation. Oh, she had no doubt of her love for Stan, or indeed, his love for her. For weeks now, she had longed to belong to him in the fullest way. He had been the first man she'd loved, she knew now that he would be the last. In her bones, she knew that Stan had never loved anyone but herself.

She squeezed his hand and, like her, he needed to be reassured.

'Everything's just fine.'

She smiled at him sideways and asked where they were going. His voice was gentle as he spoke.

'I've thought and thought about it, well, you know what about. Anyway, since I just couldn't have you embarrassed by going to some hotel, well darling, I've thought of something which I think will be ideal. Anyway, you can tell me what you think.'

Rose shook her head and laughed.

'For heaven's sake, tell me... you've really got me wondering!'

His voice was low but she caught the words.

'In the old days, when my parents married they lived over the shop. I was actually born in the flat at the top of the printing works.'

She interrupted him smiling, 'Is that where we're going? Oh Stan, it sounds marvellous!'

He relaxed visibly.

'I've had the cleaner in and bought one or two extras as the place was in a bit of a state. Still, now it's clean and habitable there. At least we won't have to worry about seeing people we know. It's somewhere private and a special place we can truly call our own.'

Chapter IX

They reached Hexham and Stan drove round to the rear of the printing works. The back lane was an off the beaten track area of the town. Should his car be seen where he had parked it, no-one would give it a second thought. It would only be assumed that his usual parking spot in a nearby side street had been used by some casual motorist.

He took her hand and helped Rose out of the car before locking it. He led her to a somewhat dingy, green, painted door. Once inside, they walked up seemingly endless stairs. At last they reached the top and Stan unlocked yet another door. The flat consisted of a large sitting room, a small kitchen with a bathroom and toilet leading off and two bedrooms.

The entire flat was furnished in the style of the twenties. As Stan had said, everywhere was shining clean. As soon as she entered, Rose noticed one of the extras Stan had mentioned. It was a large electric fire which stood in front of the old fashioned grate, looking quite out of place.

Going through to the largest of the bedrooms, Rose found a brass bedstead which was so large that at least four people could have slept in it comfortably. The bed had been made up with new sheets, pillows and a white candlewick cover. In the centre was a heavily embroidered silk rose.

Stan followed her and coughed.

'Well?'

Rose turned and flung her arms around him.

'Oh, darling. It's perfect! If this place was where your parents were happy, and they would have been married, then I can't think of a better place for you and I to have as a...'

She giggled.

'Well, I was going to say a love nest.'

After a moment, Stan went to the window, closed the curtains and switched on the electric fire. The room was immediately suffused in a soft warming glow. He then turned to Rose and put his arms around her. His voice was thick as he spoke.

'I know this place isn't exactly...'

She shushed him and smiled.

'Darling Stan, you couldn't have chosen anywhere better. When your parents came here as newlyweds, they must have been gloriously happy. This room, especially, must hold such happy memories. Let's add our pleasure to theirs; I love you, my darling. Always have and always will.'

He kissed her and for both of them, the world outside their nearness dimmed. A moment later, he released her, slipped into the next room and returned with a silver salver on which stood a bottle of champagne and two tall glasses. Having drunk most of the sparkling liquid, they smiled into each other's eyes.

As Rose replaced her glass on the salver, she noticed a small blue velvet box. Stan nodded towards it and curiously picked it up.

Rose gave a gasp as she opened the tiny lid.

'Oh Stan, oh, it's beautiful.'

Rose gazed at the sparkling gems set in the fine gold ring. She raised her eyes to his.

'Not nearly as lovely as you. I'd like to be able to give you the world,' she whispered.

'As it is, all I can offer you is my heart,' he sighed.

Laying down the box, Rose reached out and held him near. Her words filled him with a joy he had thought never to experience again.

'Just to discover that you were still alive was wonderful and to find that you still loved me, oh Stan, that was more to me than anything in the world. No matter what happens in the future, nothing will ever be as precious to me, as hearing you say, "I love you."'

They kissed again and this time, he started to undress her. It seemed to Rose that the outside world dimmed and they were engulfed in a tide of joyous passion.

The afternoon passed on wings of butterfly lightness. As Rose realised, at last, that she must leave, she sighed and opened her eyes.

Stan was gazing at her, his expression full of love. His voice was low as he spoke.

'You look exactly as you did all those years ago. You have eyes, which have always held me. Always have, always will.'

Then they smiled at one another, that special spark of deeply felt real love was like a living thing between them. One last kiss and then they got up and began to dress.

When ready and about to leave, Stan spoke quietly.

'Darling, I know its wrong, but I can't bear to think of you going back to...'

She put a finger to his lips.

'Sh... sh... darling. It's difficult for both of us. It can't be anything else. At least we did find each other again. Let's just be grateful for that. When we have our special times, we'll just have to learn to switch off from the real world and when we have to return to it, well Stan, that's what we'll have to do.'

Her voice broke off and, at once, Stan tried to reassure her. With his hands on her shoulders, he faced her.

'You're right, of course. What's ours is ours for as long as we have it. Beyond that, well we've just got to do the best we can.'

They looked at each other for a long moment, then, Rose spoke gently.

'There is nothing either of us can do to lessen our responsibilities. You have to keep a stable home for your son. Fifteen is an impressionable age. I have no worries about Iris as she loves working for you, and is not only pretty and popular, but she is beginning to take an interest in boys. The day will come when she will marry and have a home of her own.'

Her voice stopped and then she heaved a big sigh. Stan looked at her and knew she was thinking of her son. Her tone was sad as she went on.

'Poor darling David. He'll need me for as long as he lives. As he gets older, he only becomes stronger and there is little chance of any improvement mentally.'

She raised her eyes and Stan winced at the sadness in them. Her next words came as a surprise.

'As for Ben, well, he was good enough to marry me, give his name to someone else's child, and how was he repaid? When his own son was born, the son he had longed for, was cruelly afflicted with an illness which would not only seriously affect his abilities but end his life much sooner than normal.'

Stan drew her to him and for a moment, they clung close. Then, pulling herself up, Rose gave him a watery smile and made for the door.

'Come on, time for the real world. Let's go.'

As their journey back to their real worlds unfolded, Stan spoke.

'I've been thinking about what you said back there. Rose, all these years you've been undermining yourself. You can take it from me, Ben Carter did himself a far better favour by marrying you than you realise.'

She looked surprised.

'No, listen to me. You told me yourself that he asked for your money as soon as you were married. Alright, so it was for your mutual benefit in the small-holding, but, has he ever offered you anything in return?'

She shook her head.

'No, I thought not. He must have thought his ship really had come in when he realised the situation.'

Rose bit her lip. Her voice had a catch in it as she whispered, 'Stan, you must remember I was pregnant with your child. He gave her a name and gave me some respectability.'

'He fell on his feet when he married you. There he was, not fit for the Forces, kicked out of his job when the old girl died. Alright, so he had a bit of a small-holding but without you and your money, he'd have been on the scrap heap in no time,' Stan's voice was bitter as he replied.

'Understand this, Rose. That awful husband of yours hasn't even the sense to be pleasant, never mind try to make you happy. Remember this, Rose... he might be your husband but that doesn't give him the right to hound you at every turn.'

As they reached the point where she must alight, Stan wished that he had held his tongue. The man was a miserable, uneducated lout, but, after all, he was her husband. Perhaps in the beginning it had all been for the best. Who knows, she might even have felt something for him in those days.

He watched as she hurried lightly under the high hedge and turned in at the twisty lane. He sat for a moment savouring the sweetness of the last few hours. He wondered how long they could go on living a lie with their partners, and loving each other the way they did. As he drove home, little did he realise just how soon he would have to face up to gossip.

*

Months passed and the weekly trip to the little flat at the top of the printing works became a regular habit. The love between Rose and Stan never lessened or wavered, and they gave each other a special strength to face the partings which they both faced.

Miss Pierce sighed as she put down his usual cup of rum tea and lightly touched his shoulder. This brought to light the gossip which she had tried hard to put down.

Stan glanced at his trusty secretary. Her voice was friendly as he asked her to take a cup with him. He knew her well and suspected she had something awkward to say, so Stan asked her if there was anything on her mind.

She swallowed hard and looked at him straight in the eye. She took a deep breath and her voice was gentle, but firm, as she spoke.

'I'm sorry Mr Bailey, you know I only speak out of respect and the fact that I care very much about... how life is for you.'

Stan breathed a little quicker. She'd heard something – he knew it – he leaned forward and knew that she had very high morals and cared that people should be honest and caring of each other. He looked at her expectantly.

'Yesterday, I had cause to go up into the binding department,' Miss Pierce gave a little cough then went on.

'Whilst there, I happened to overhear a comment. A comment, Mr Bailey, which is doing the rounds of the entire works, I am sorry to say.'

Stan's voice was tense.

'Oh yes?'

'Yes. I'm afraid there is talk about yourself and a... well, a lady. It seems your car has been seen at the rear somewhat regularly and well... I thought you should know as gossip soon spreads. It would be dreadful if...'

She looked at him. Whatever her boss was up to she didn't care, just so long as no trouble came to him because of it. He was a man of great stature in her eyes, a man done down by an uncaring wife and an ungrateful country. Let anyone do or say what they would against him as she, Julia Pierce, who had seen him grow from boyhood, would defend him to the end, whatever it took. At this moment, she felt the motherly feeling which she had always felt for this man and reached out and touched his hand.

Stan felt the caring aura sweep over him. He knew in his heart that this woman was to be trusted. He looked at her and his trust was implicit.

'Miss Pierce, would you like my confidence or would you prefer not to know? You see, I feel as if I could tell you anything... but if hearing a confession would upset you, I...'

Miss Pierce was covering his hand with her own. She had been a romantic novel reader for years. The thousands of words, telling tales of pride, passion, lust, desire and hate, usually held her spellbound. Blinking in stunned silence, she listened to her employer.

In a quiet voice, at times almost breaking with sadness, Stan told of his war-time meeting with Rose. He described their air raid entombment and eventual rescue. He told her how they had had to part, almost immediately, and how, as so often happened in war-time, the wrong information had been put out and lives had been disrupted.

As the tale unfolded, Miss Pierce sat with goose-pimples breaking out as she heard of Rose, not only finding herself pregnant, but also out on a limb, with no family to help her and few real friends. Many had been the books she had read, even more, the films she had sat and wept through, none, however, touched her as deeply as did the real life story of her employer and his beloved Rose.

As Stan finished talking, he gave her a quizzical glance. Her eyes were staring at him and her voice was full of sadness as she spoke.

'Oh, Mr Bailey. How sad, how perfectly dreadful.'

A sudden thought struck her and her eyes widened.

Iris!

She looked at the closed door on the other side of which the result of this sad drama sat typing, blissfully unaware that her natural father had, for the first time in his life, told anyone that he had a daughter.

Miss Pierce heaved a sigh and realised it was little wonder that her boss looked a bit strained these days. However, if anything, she was more determined than ever that whatever it took, be it a white lie or a downright black untruth, she would defend his good name to her last breath.

She sighed and stood up. Her current Mills and Boon, full of wonders of love and romance, had nothing on this real life drama. Looking at her boss, her face and voice were gentle as she spoke.

'If at any time you need me, in any way whatsoever, please, *please* do not hesitate to call upon my services.'

She could have wept at his look which was full of gratitude and, yes, she felt sure that he was looking at her with an affection which only they understood.

She went round the desk and touched his shoulder.

'You can rely on me, Mr Bailey. I'll take the matter in hand, tell you what, I'll drop a few hints about you writing a book about the world of printing through the ages. I'll mention that if any of the work-force would like to offer any comments on printing, or have any amusing anecdotes to offer, they can come and discuss them with you.'

Stan sighed with relief. His secretary was solid gold right through. Who else but Miss Pierce would have been so prepared to offer such backup? He smiled approvingly.

'Dad always said you were a treasure. I've always known it, of course, and don't know what the old man would have said about this situation.'

His voice tailed off and Miss Pierce broke in.

'Given all the facts, he would be first to understand, just as…' – she gave a little cough – 'just as I do my dear, just as I do.'

She quickly and silently left his side and slipped through the door.

*

Cara Bailey sat at her dressing table. She drummed her long finger nails on the polished walnut top. She could sense there was something up and had felt it for some time. Furrowing her brow, she tried to think.

For weeks – no it was months – she felt her husband had been different. He had come into the house whistling and had seemed preoccupied. He never upset her in any way – he wouldn't dare. She stopped drumming and looked in the mirror. He had changed recently. He seemed happy about something.

As she gazed at herself, a thought struck her, which she dismissed immediately. However, like an aching tooth, the thought persisted. In all of their married life, Stan had never given her a moment's doubt regarding his fidelity. Their marriage might leave a lot to be desired and Cara knew, in her heart, that her constant demands for the latest fashions in furniture, dresses and expensive holidays, took every penny that he made. Still, it was all his fault. If he had sold up and taken her to live in London, which he could have done, then she would have enjoyed life in the swinging capital, instead of wasting away in this holier than thou, rural community.

Cara smiled to herself. She had, of course, one or two friends, who, like herself, kicked over the traces now and again. She smiled and agreed that there had been times when the memory of a tall, blonde Swede, whose accent she had fallen for, returned to her. They had enjoyed a wild time in his boat on the Norfolk Broads. Of course, this was all a long time ago. Still, a woman had to have her secrets – didn't they all?

Cara mused about her husband. He was dull and lived for that damned printing works. If he had ever thought about an affair, and Cara doubted it, when would he have had the time? How could he afford to wine and dine some floozy? No, he might be up to something - but an affair – never! Her mind went to Eric who was a good-looking boy. He was not such a boy these days but more a charming young man. She smiled – her feelings for Stan might have waned long ago but she loved her son.

She thought about the rapport between Stan and Eric. From day one, Stan had been a great father. Through school days, he had walked and talked with his son and now, although he could have stayed on at school, Eric had wanted, above all, to be trained up for the family business.

He now worked under the eagle eye of that old witch, Miss Pierce. Cara sniffed. Stan had never given a thought to getting rid of her. Good heavens, he could have had a swinging secretary years ago, but no, he had clung on to old Miss Pepper. Cara laughed at her own pet name for Miss Pierce. Well, if she needed proof that Stan was too miserable to have an affair, she need look no further than old Pepper. They deserved each other – old Pepper and old misery guts.

However, the nagging doubt about Stan and his happier outlook these days irked her. He didn't deserve to be happy. Nobody who lived for work and a damned garden, was worthy of a second thought. Anyway, she was determined to find out what was going on. She still held the purse strings, so it couldn't be costing much. She'd find out, if just to have a good laugh over it. She'd knock that silly look off his face – now that *would* be a laugh!

Chapter X

She quickly realised that she had been boringly good lately and agreed that this house was far too big for her to keep it up to scratch. Admittedly, she did have Dora who came in once a month to *do through* as the old girl called it. Still, a lot of work was required to be done by Cara for the place to be kept in good order.

Cara furrowed her brow again. What was the name of that agency in town which hired out domestics by the day? She remembered they were called Merry Maids – she would need their services if she was going to have some time to herself and find out what Stan was up to. A skivvy for a couple of days in the next few weeks would be a godsend.

She arranged that the following Monday morning, she would have the services of one of the best domestic workers that Merry Maids had to offer – Miss Jenny Briggs.

Iris was now almost eighteen and she and Eric worked in harmony under the eagle eye of Miss Pierce. Eric was younger than Iris by nearly two years which slightly amused her. It was nice to have the son of the manager asking her to help him with things now and again. He might be a little younger than she, but, somehow he always seemed older.

Like Iris, he had an ear for languages. He went to night school to study but Iris, having learnt to speak French from childhood with her mother, often helped him with his grammar.

He had found out about her proficiency in French in a somewhat embarrassing way. When, as is the way with callow young men, he had tried to impress Iris with his reading of a French menu which the firm was printing, he stumbled on some of the pronunciations, and she had come over to his desk, leaned over his shoulder and in a perfect accent, had read out the complete menu. The result had been laughter from every corner of the office. Even Miss Pierce had smiled indulgently at the giggling pair. He admired her and whispered that he wouldn't mind her helping him with his homework, which she agreed to. Miss Pierce thought it a good thing, and encouraged them to carry on the good work of improving their knowledge of everything they could as she often said, "knowledge is no burden".

Stan heard the laughter from the Manager's Office and came out. As Eric explained, Stan smiled at Iris and murmured, forgetting for the moment the need for constant care.

His voice was quite natural as he spoke.

'Oh yes, your mother was an excellent linguist as I recall.'

Seeing the sudden warning look from Miss Pierce, as well as the astonished glance as Iris looked at him open mouthed, he realised his blunder and quickly made a joke of it.

His voice had a slight catch in it as he tried to speak lightly.

'During the war, I was in the Navy and your mother was in the WRENS. Met her once and she amazed us all with her terrific ability with languages, all a long time ago, of course. Still, nice to know you take after her.'

With a little cough, he slipped back into his own office, leaving behind him an amazed son and an equally amazed Iris.

Only Miss Pierce had any idea of how he must be feeling. Inside, she ached for him and thought it best to let him have a minute to pull himself together. She'd see that these two were kept too busy for gossip, or have time to think about that slip of the tongue.

She set them to work and she slipped into the inner office where she found Stan sitting with his hands covering his face. With a tiny sigh, she set about making a cup of strong rum tea.

His look was a little sheepish as he glanced at her.

'Do you think there'll be any come-backs? The words just slipped out.'

He shook his head.

Miss Pierce smiled and assured him that all would have now been forgotten as she had given them plenty to do.

She gave a little smile and confirmed that they would have no time for chit chat due to the amount of work she had given to them. Stan nodded – his look was all the thanks Miss Pierce needed as she left the office quietly.

Jenny Briggs sat on the bus taking her towards Hexham. As the lovely countryside sped past, she thought about her life. From childhood she'd had to slave, scrimp and scratch for a living. The war had come when she was in her early twenties and work was available in factories, shops and indeed any and every place where women were able to be employed. With so many of them in the forces, labour was gladly taken on when offered.

Jenny had hit lucky, when that rich old girl up at the lodge wanted a live-in housekeeper. Jenny had presented herself as locally born, no ties and happy to live in. She landed herself a job she liked and a job in which she could feel a pride and most of all, a job which just might, if she played her cards right, leave her with a home that her sister would envy and something she could never hope to match, however long she might work. It was all a very big 'if' of course. Still, as long as she stayed and worked hard, the old girl might just leave her the house in her Will.

It was an added joy when Ben Carter was taken on as gardener. They had both been born in the area and, in their younger teenage days, been known to dance together at local hops. Jenny Briggs had certainly made up her mind about what she wanted out of life – she wanted to be mistress of High Copperas Lodge, but above all, she wanted to marry Ben Carter and share it with him. Oh wouldn't she just cock a snoot at that snobbish, spiteful sister of hers when she was both mistress of a fine house and wife of a big strong man like Ben Carter.

As it turned out, she had achieved neither. This so embittered her that she secretly took a nip of gin. This in turn did help her to sleep but it also became a need.

When Copperas Lodge was sold, Jenny had to move out. Grinding her teeth, she moved back in with her sister and brother-in-law. Skivying after them was a torment. All she ever received for running after them, day in and day out was bed, board and a few grudging pounds each month.

However, one day she went to town and saw a large notice: 'Domestic Workers Needed, Apply Within'. At once she went through the swing doors, climbed a wide flight of stairs and saw in front of her, a smart door with the title Merry Maids Inc. The greeting she received put her at ease. The outcome, she was told, was that she was put on their books, only for a month as a trial period. She smiled – they needn't worry, she might be little and a bit on the dumpy side, but by God, whatever else she might not be able to do, she could do anything in a house. Oh yes, Jenny was soon an accepted member of the Merry Maids Inc workforce.

Because of this, she was able to gather her few possessions together and give her sister a most unsisterly farewell. It was a delighted and gloating Jenny Briggs, who became a tenant of her very own bedsitter. It was only a short walk from the town centre. She spent nothing on fares as the firm paid for journeys to and from the many and varied homes which they sent their workers to.

Loneliness, however, is a terrible thing. After long days of scrubbing and cleaning other people's homes, Jenny returned to her drab little room in comparison to the homes which she worked in and thought about how it might have been, had she not let that snooty bitch, Rose Bamber, snip Ben Carter from under her very nose.

At such times, Jenny would slip out to the off-licence and buy a bottle of gin. Lying on the bed, she would splash the gin into her glass, sometimes sip it, but at others, would gulp it down. It only helped to enhance her feelings of resentment against a world which, in her eyes, had treated her badly. It also helped to feed the hatred she knew she would always feel towards that damned uppity bitch who had stolen her man. Her usual last jumbled thoughts were a mixture of meeting up with that fancy pants piece, giving her what she so justly deserved, and last, but by no means least, somehow walking away into the sunset with Ben Carter.

One morning after a bad night and with a hangover, she felt like anything but work. She rose and went to Merry Maids Inc almost like an automaton. It was with a mixture of surprise and pleasure that she accepted the job at Hexham. If nothing else, the journey would be pleasant and the time involved in travelling, would be less time on her knees scrubbing and cleaning.

Alighting at the bus station in Hexham, Jenny made an enquiry and set off down the main street. At a rather smart shop she stopped and looked in the window. At the back was a mirror and she glanced at her reflection and as she did so, she gasped... There, right alongside her own was another, and... Oh, God... it couldn't be, but it was... it was Rose Bamber.

Just as quickly it was gone, Jenny felt her legs go weak. Dear God, she was seeing things now. She turned to look all around her but all she saw was the rear view of a teenager, all legs and mini-skirt. It couldn't possibly be that bitch, surely not. By now she'd be a worn out hag – that sort couldn't take to a working class existence and still stay madam-like and pretty. Jenny Briggs tried to pull herself together as she had a job to do and felt it best to get on with it, as she would have time for dreaming later. Slipping her hand into her pocket, she pulled out her agency card. The name and address on it was Mrs Bailey, 22 Turret Square, Hexham. She quickly made off in the direction she had been given.

In his office, Stan Bailey listened to what Miss Pierce was saying with mounting horror. Her voice was low and filled with concern as she ended.

'So you do see Mr Bailey, why I had to speak to you about it?'

He nodded wearily, dear God in heaven, why hadn't he foreseen the danger of such a thing happening? Two young people like Eric and Iris, both with similar interests, working in a close environment, thrown together, her coaching him in French? Only the other week he had smiled as he found them practising dance steps during the dinner hour. For some reason he had never given the good rapport between the two a second thought. He groaned inwardly, *hell's flames*, something would have to be done – they were, after all, half brother and sister, without knowing it.

He looked at Miss Pierce and her face had a worried, sad look. No wonder, as only a short time ago she had caught them in the act of kissing in the walk-in stationery cupboard. It hadn't been a quick peck either. Miss Pierce felt her face flush as she described what she had seen. Not a fun sort of kiss in passing, it was indeed a passionate kiss, a lover's kiss, and this was why she had felt it necessary to inform her beloved employer. Miss Pierce had shuddered and was certain that, at all costs, everyone must be saved from the troublesome possibility of incest.

Stan stood up and felt the matter had to be discussed with Rose at the earliest possible moment. Thank God that mean husband had had the telephone installed. Now, always that extra bit careful, he asked Miss Pierce to make the call which she did and, as Rose answered, she handed the receiver to Stan and quietly left him to it.

Rose had a raging toothache. She had woken in the early hours and gone into the kitchen for some aspirin.

When she returned, Ben had stirred.

'What's up?' he mumbled.

'Toothache, the whole left side of my face is throbbing. I've just taken some aspirin.'

Her low voice took on a sharp edge, 'For God's sake, let me try and get some sleep.'

He turned away – it wasn't his fault if she had toothache. It wasn't his fault if she couldn't sleep and wondered why she always made everything seem to be his fault. He settled down to letting his mind dwell on all his wife's faults.

The first spark of unfairness he had felt began to dart about in his mind. It picked up other sparks and they mingled, enlarging and multiplying. By morning, a fireball of mixed resentment and frustration pushed about in his brain. He rose earlier than usual and, after only a banana instead of his usual full breakfast, he stamped out of the house to attack that bad patch in the big field.

He stabbed at the brown earth and glanced up as it looked like rain. The gathering black clouds matched exactly how he felt. Again, he jabbed at the earth. His expression was grim and his face twisted. He felt a little lightheaded. Of course, he hadn't had any breakfast but whose fault was that? It was the fault of that smart wife of his who was lying in bed instead of looking after him. His mood was the blackest and heaviest he had ever known.

Rose hurried to answer the telephone – its ring always set David off kicking and banging. She sighed as she heard Stan speak at the other end and felt it was wonderful to hear his voice just when she felt so wretched. The left side of her face was swollen and flushed. Whatever was wrong was more than toothache and, for this reason, she had decided to call in to the afternoon surgery and see the doctor.

'Can you talk?' Stan's voice was as caring as ever, but Rose caught the hidden anxiety.

'Yes, Ben's down in the big field. What is it Stan, you sound worried?'

'Not over the phone. Is it possible to meet as we have to talk?'

Rose made up her mind that Stan was worried and it could only be about one thing. She took a quick sharp breath and pain shot through her face.

'Yes, of course, I have to call in at the surgery this afternoon.'

Her voice took on a nervous note and Stan caught it.

'I'll have to push the wheelchair to the main street in the village. Meet me in the Brass Kettle you know, the little tea-shop, it won't cause gossip as whenever I go in there, someone always helps me with the wheelchair and nobody will think twice about a little courtesy.'

'Look, if it's too...'

Stan didn't get any further, Rose interrupted him quickly.

'No Stan, I've had a rotten night that's all. Seeing you will cheer me up. Honestly.'

'Only if you're sure, then,' he said.

Stan couldn't bear to think of Rose pushing that heavy wheelchair. However, he would be glad to see her. God, how could he expect her to have a ready answer to the problem?

'I'll be in the teashop from two o'clock. See you later then, darling.'

At the other end of the line, Rose tried to smile but the effort caused her even more pain. What a mess her face was in and she hoped Stan wouldn't get too much of a shock when they met.

She gently whispered into the telephone.

'See you later, my love. See you as soon as I can.'

She quietly replaced the receiver and went to get ready.

Cara Bailey was pleased enough with her new domestic worker. There was however, something about the woman which actually gave her the creeps from time to time. There was no doubt she was a good worker and she never wasted a drop of soapy water. Just as soon as the washing was done, Jenny would go out into the back garden where the roses and paths would be given a refreshing drink.

For the first few days of Jenny coming to work for her, Cara stayed at home and watched her closely. It didn't do to trust anyone these days. Just look at that husband of hers – he didn't mention anything happening which might give cause for pleasure, yet these days he whistled about the place and seemed forever in a state of happy contentment.

Cara questioned Eric and he could offer no explanation. Orders at the Works were pretty much the same and it seemed to Cara that Eric was just as potty about the place as Stan. What was it about that damned printing works which drew them both? How could a noisy, grimy place like that hold interest for anyone?

Jenny had been working for Cara for just over two weeks when she suddenly let slip her hatred for another woman. Cara chuckled to herself. So, the little oddity, as Cara privately described Jenny, had once been in love and had been jilted. How anyone could have ever found her attractive was a mystery to Cara. Jenny was now a short, shapeless and grey-haired creature. Her clothes were obviously second-hand and she walked with a kind of hurrying shuffle. Cara couldn't imagine that even in her youth, Jenny would have had any attraction.

However, Cara now had other things on her mind. If her husband was up to anything, she intended to find out about it. This afternoon, she would pay his office a flying, unannounced visit. That always made his jaw drop and as for that pepper-pot of a secretary, well, she could jolly well put up with being nice to the wife of her boss.

Cara had no illusions as to how Miss Pierce regarded her. In the old days when she had been a junior in the office, Cara had had to put up with Miss Pierce as her superior. Well, now old pepper-pot would have no option but to be pleasant and obliging towards her.

Cara set off for the office. It was an unfortunate coincidence that the day she chose, was the same day that Stan had arranged to meet Rose in the teashop.

Chapter XI

As she left, Cara had no real idea as to just what she expected. The thought of Stan caring for someone else, gave her a sudden rush. It amazed her. Good God, she hadn't loved Stan for years and wondered why she felt like this. Cara suddenly understood. It came as a shock that she could feel jealous and she hadn't any illusions as to her feelings for Stan. For years now she had only tolerated him but was that really all? After all, she had been mad about him in the beginning, had set her cap at him until she got him and now, what had happened?

Cara knew what had happened. She had become bored as Stan had had to work like a slave in the business. His own uncle had ridden roughshod over him. Cara had expected Stan to fight for his rights but instead, he had given in when the Works was eventually left to Cara and not to Stan, as promised. He had simply shrugged and carried on. His excuse was that one day it would really belong to a Bailey and their son, Eric, would inherit. After all, it was he who put his heart and soul into making Bailey's Printing Works a good, sound and profitable business.

Stan shrugged into his coat and, watched by Miss Pierce, left the building. It saddened her to see his steps so heavy and how downcast he seemed.

His mind was now churning and he felt he shouldn't have contacted Rose so quickly, as it would have been far better to have given the matter some thought. How on earth could she be expected to come up with an answer? He wondered what had possessed him to think the matter was so urgent that it couldn't wait for a few days.

As he nosed the car out of the busy market town, he thought of Rose struggling towards the village main street with the heavy wheelchair. He thought of her waiting for him and trying to appear casual when they met.

What had she said on the telephone? Oh yes, she had to go to the village anyway, had to see the doctor about something – was it herself or David? Stan couldn't think what she had actually said.

At last, he pulled up outside the Brass Kettle where he found Rose sitting at a corner table. He bought a cup of coffee and looked round casually. There were one or two other empty tables. Nevertheless, he made a beeline for the corner.

Cara Bailey arrived at the printing works about five minutes after her husband had left. Miss Pierce managed a smile of welcome and the offer of a cup of tea or coffee. Cara levelled a look at her. The old witch hadn't changed much – she still went about with an air of bossiness, which grated on Cara.

With a somewhat lofty look and tartness in her tone, she answered the elderly woman.

'I haven't come for tea, Miss Pierce. I've called to see my husband. Now, will you tell him I'm here or shall I surprise him?'

Miss Pierce swallowed hard. She disliked this jumped-up little madam but felt there was nothing for it but to make her welcome and seem pleased to do so.

'I'm sorry Mrs Bailey, but your husband had to go out on business… something about deliveries, I think.' Her voice held a mild regret as she answered. Miss Pierce hoped and prayed that she sounded convincing. Her voice changed ever so slightly as she added, 'He didn't mention to me that you were expected...'

'I only decided at lunchtime to make a call. Well, since he isn't here and you cannot tell me where he is, I may as well have a word with my son if you don't mind,' Cara broke in snappishly.

Miss Pierce led Cara through from the outer entrance. As they passed one of the desks, Miss Pierce stopped beside a pretty young girl with a bright smile who quickly looked up.

'This is Miss Carter, Mrs Bailey, she has been with the firm nearly three years and is doing very well. We are all pleased with her progress.'

The young girl stood up and extended her hand and as Cara shook it, she studied the face and figure of the teenager. If she was being praised by old pepper-pot, she must be working like a slave!

At that moment, Eric came through the door and greeted his mother with some surprise.

'Hello, mum. Didn't know you were coming in today.'

Cara turned and looked at her son. He was standing quite close to the tall pretty office junior. They did make a handsome pair. Cara noted the glance which passed between them. So what, no doubt Eric was sowing wild oats, and why not? Didn't all young men?

Eric glanced at his mother, he knew for a fact that she hadn't been expected and he had no idea where his father had gone off to so unexpectedly. Still, he knew the direction he had taken. He spoke quite innocently and Miss Pierce felt her throat go dry as he did so.

'Don't know where Dad went off to. Perhaps to Prudhoe or Rigton, as we do have business in both towns. Anyway, he took the road down past the hospital so he must be going to one or the other.'

He stopped and glanced at both his mother and Iris, and his tone had an admiring sound which Cara did not miss.

'We're thinking of entering Iris for the Trainee Secretary of the Year award, mum. Miss Pierce can vouch for her work and I certainly think she looks the part.'

The girl sat down quickly and began to type. Cara smiled to herself; her son knew how to charm – quite a chip off the old block in that respect. With one of her secret smiles, Cara took hold of her son by the arm.

'Tell you what, no point in my stopping if your father's not here, you can walk me down to the taxi rank and I'll see you both tonight.'

So saying, Cara gave a smiling glance at Iris and without so much as a nod at Miss Pierce, she swept out of the building.

They walked towards the taxi rank, which nestled so well alongside the abbey grounds and opposite the well run Beaumont Hotel.

'Does your father go out very often at lunch times? I mean, does he go anywhere for a regular meal?' Cara asked lightly.

Eric laughed.

'Good heavens, no. In fact, Dad and I quite often have a pint and a pie down the pub.'

Cara raised an eyebrow and her son chuckled.

'Well, Dad has a Guinness and I have a ginger ale,' he added.

Cara smiled, 'I should think so too.'

She gave her son a sideways glance.

'And what about Miss Mini Skirt? You two seem to have a lot in common!'

Eric suddenly seemed very serious. His voice held an admiration which was not lost on Cara.

'Iris is great, mum. Not only can she do almost everything in the office, she's so quick at everything and even speaks two other languages with a super accent. She's helping me with my French.'

He stopped and Cara smiled again to herself. Handing his mother into a taxi he straightened up, stood for a second, then as the cab moved off, he turned and made his way back to the office.

As Cara's taxi reached a roundabout, Cara spoke suddenly.

'Take the Rigton road, please.'

Why had she said that and what was it that Eric had said earlier? Oh yes, his father had gone to either Prudhoe or Rigton. Cara could never recall any mention of Prudhoe but she could remember a long time ago that one day her husband had walked in with a bag of vegetables, he had laid them on the kitchen table saying he had picked them up in Rigton.

As the taxi neared the village, Cara kept a sharp look out. Rounding a corner into the main street, she saw what she was looking for, which was her husband's car and it was parked outside a small café.

The village main street was not as busy as usual. From first light, heavy clouds had amassed, looking dark and threatening. She paid her taxi fare and walked along towards the café.

What she saw made her draw back a little. Stan was sitting at a corner table with a woman and a boy in a wheelchair. As her eyes fell on the woman's face, Cara shuddered and muttered.

'Oh God, how awful to be born with a face like that.'

She looked at the wheelchair again and felt sympathy for anyone having a child like that. David was sticking out his tongue, kicking his legs aimlessly and his eyes were rolling round as if out of control, which indeed they were.

As Cara edged towards the window, she noticed Stan was obviously speaking very earnestly to the woman who appeared to be trying to hide the worst side of her face. She felt there was no doubt about it – the woman and the boy in the wheelchair were definitely freaks. What business her husband had with these people, Cara couldn't hazard a guess. One thing was for sure, it could hardly be an affair of the heart, not with that woman and her terrible face.

A sudden gust of wind brought with it a lash of heavy raindrops. Glancing round, Cara noticed that the car was unlocked and she didn't expect Stan to be much longer, so decided to wait in the car until he came out. It wouldn't be him wanting an explanation – it would be her! As Cara quickly turned away, her high heel became caught in a crevice and she crashed to the ground.

At the sound of the commotion, Stan looked up and was shocked to see his wife lying in the rain which almost unnerved him. He rose and from the door he whispered, 'It's Cara. I must see to her.'

He went out quickly and with the help of a lone passerby, assisted his wife into the café. As Cara was helped into a seat and quickly given a cup of tea by the pleasant woman behind the counter, Rose felt her face flush. How embarrassing to be found in a café with someone else's husband and by the wife at that! She just couldn't face anything other than a brief introduction. Looking at her watch, she realised that the surgery would now be open.

Stan helped her out of the door with the wheelchair. His expression was now quite relaxed.

'Don't worry, I'll deal with everything. Just you get yourself well again. Ring me tomorrow at work, promise?'

With a slight nod – it was all she could manage – Rose set off down the main street.

Having bought two more teas, Stan sat down opposite his wife and, as Cara took a drink, he decided to get in first.

'There now, you look lots better. So, just what the hell do you think you are up to?'

His tone was edgy as he spoke. He leaned forward and looked her in the eye.

'Apart from spying on your husband.'

Cara blinked and hadn't expected this. If anything, she was the one who should be asking the questions and she had looked forward to demanding explanations, not being questioned herself.

Swallowing hard, she tried to think. Before coming out today, instead of her usual coffee and sandwiches, she'd had a couple of large vodkas. Taking a glass into the kitchen, she had found the little oddity with a bottle of gin. It obviously belonged to the woman and, having been caught out drinking on the job, she had asked Cara to join her. She now felt a little fuddled.

Well, she might be just a little tight, but she wasn't a fool. God, but she felt terrible. Still, she hadn't done anything wrong lately. However, she rounded in on Stan and her voice was high and petulant.

'Spying? *Spying*... and remember... it was your word not mine. But, if the cap fits...'

She shook her head.

'Anyway, what about that woman and that dreadful child? What business do you have with freaks like that?'

Stan felt a rush of something akin to rage which almost consumed him. He couldn't understand how in God's name anyone could call a child a freak. He realised, not for the first time, how little he really knew his wife.

He looked at her and decided to quietly tell as much of the truth as would suffice for the moment.

'That woman who left just now...'

'Yes, yes. You said her name was Carter,' Cara snapped.

'That's right and that was her son in the wheelchair.'

Cara stared at him.

'Well?'

Stan swallowed hard.

'We have a young girl in the office. A very pretty young girl...'

Again Cara broke in.

'Oh, I know that. I called there today. Met her as a matter of fact. Very pretty as you say. Mind you, too much leg and not enough skirt if you ask me. So what?'

Stan stared at her.

Although he appreciated that Rose and David hadn't looked themselves today, he felt it wasn't the right time for Rose to have any further trouble.

'You say you were at the office? And you met young Iris?'

He leaned closer.

'Did you notice how close she and Eric have become?'

Cara was trying to work out what he was getting at, as he seemed very serious about something. For the life of her, she just could not put her finger on it. She shrugged and Stan continued

'The woman who left earlier was Mrs Carter, the girl in our office is Iris Carter, the boy in the wheelchair is her brother. Our son Eric is very keen on Iris, now do you understand what I'm doing here?'

'Oh, my God! That lovely girl is related to those... oh, Stan.'

Cara looked horrified.

'We must get Eric away from her... oh, God.

She felt the need of a good stiff drink. Her clothes were filthy and wet, her shoes were ruined.

'Get me home, for God's sake,' she muttered sharply.
'I'll have a bath. You see to Eric and I'll see to myself.'

Stan took his wife by the arm and led her outside to the car. The rain was lashing down and the sky had a menacing look about it.

On the way home Cara acknowledged that she now understood the reason for Stan being in Rigton. Naturally, like her, he'd want to investigate any family that Eric might wish to marry into. Of course, he was much too young to be thinking along those lines. Still, Stan had done the right thing and, once Eric saw what the girl's family were like, he would soon look in another direction.

Cara asked Stan if he had ever been to Rigton before and he admitted that the first time he had ever been there was for petrol when he saw a woman at the pumps with vegetables. When he admired them she said they were on sale at a spot further on. Stan glanced at his wife and she was taking in what he was saying so he went on.

'It's years ago now but I brought a bagful home and that was when I first met Mr Carter, a real brute of a man. Wouldn't want any family of mine having anything to do with him.'

Cara felt strange, as if she were watching what was happening, rather than taking part. Stan glanced at his wife who had a funny look about her. Still, not surprising, she'd had a nasty fall, not only that, but she had been caught out spying on him. Stan knew how his wife hated being the one in the wrong and never could accept that anything she said or did, deserved adverse comment.

As they arrived home, he asked her if she would be alright. Hardly able to reply, she gave him an insolent look, made a wry face and struggled out of the car. Stan sighed and, having watched her safely enter the doorway, let in the clutch and set off for the Works.

Chapter XII

Stan hurried into the office and Miss Pierce met him with a worried glance. He nodded and she followed him into the inner sanctum. Having made sure that the heavy door was shut, Stan regaled her with an account of his last two hours.

Miss Pierce felt her throat go dry as she heard of Mrs Carter and Mrs Bailey sitting in the same café. She wondered how her boss had managed the situation so well. Stan, of course, had carefully refrained from telling her how he had to use the sight of Rose with her swollen face and almost closed left eye (as well as David in his wheelchair), as an excuse for checking out the family in which his son was interested.

A short while later, Eric looked in on his father then quickly looked away. He had a feeling in his bones that there might be words between his parents tonight. He didn't want to be around so he had decided to stay in town, have a snack then go to the first house pictures with one of his mates.

'Alright son, enjoy yourself,' his father smiled.

He sighed and wondered if Iris might be the 'mate' mentioned. That problem was going to be a poser and no mistake. When he asked his secretary if she had any idea whether or not Iris was going straight home, she answered at once.

'Oh yes, she mentioned this morning that she was worried about her mother. Apparently she was going to the doctors and Iris has asked if she might go a little earlier so I know for a fact that she'll be going straight home.'

Miss Pierce saw the quick relief on Stan's face and sighed.

'Oh, wouldn't it be just wonderful if those two suddenly lost interest in each other? It happens all the time you know, young people are like that, madly in love one minute, passing strangers the next.'

They looked at each other and Stan shook his head.

'We should be so lucky.'

Miss Pierce touched his arm lightly then quickly turned and went back into the outer office.

Cara thankfully staggered through to the smart living room. Going over to the drinks cabinet, she took out a bottle of gin and reaching further in, also brought out a bottle of vodka. The vodka would not smell on her breath; she felt really awful as she had had a hell of a day. Perhaps a drink, no, better still, a *damned good* drink, would drive this internal jerkiness away. She poured herself a good glassful and swigged it down.

Jenny came through from the kitchen. The sight of Cara all muddied, with torn tights and a broken shoe caused her to hurry forward. Cara waved her away, her words were cruel and Jenny felt them hit her like sharp little stones.

'Go on, get out of my sight... you're nothing but a bloody little od... od... a bloody oddity,' she slurred.

Jenny knew that the woman was drunk, but that didn't matter, Jenny also knew that in this situation, the truth often came out.

Now, as Cara spoke again, Jenny stopped as she was about to hurry from the room.

'Iris Carter, so bloody pretty. But do you know what?'

Her head lolled from side to side as she spoke.

'Her mother is a freak, her brother is a freak and my husband had the sense for once in his life...' she hiccupped loudly, her voice dropped to a mutter and Jenny had to lean close to hear.

'Yes, Stan did right for once. I saw him talking to Mrs Carter. Oh, God. What a terrible face.'

She blinked and reached for the gin bottle.

'And oh,' she shuddered. 'That dreadful child. Worst freak I ever saw.'

As Jenny walked into the kitchen and saw her coat behind the door, she made a sudden decision to go early. So what if that drunken madam complained; she was a spiteful, nasty woman and had no right to call anyone an oddity.

Jenny suddenly felt sick of everything; sick of having to skivvy for a living, sick of all this travelling and most of all she was sick of nobody loving her. Worst of all, she hated the thought that there was no one in the whole wide world who needed her.

She collected her thoughts as she sat down. After all, Ben Carter had cared for her once. Admittedly, he had never loved her, but if that 'butter wouldn't melt' Rose Bamber hadn't snipped him from under her very nose...

She sighed as it seemed Rose was faring badly these days. She had not only turned into a freak but also had a freak child. Jenny grinned bitterly and decided she would go to Rigton. If it was Ben Carter who lived there with his family, she'd give them a call. Perhaps then he would look at her and wish he had married her instead of the woman who had turned into an ugly duckling.

Ben Carter felt light-headed and had felt strange all day. He wondered what time it was. He'd had no breakfast, apart from a banana. He had worked in the big field until his head and ears buzzed with the effort.

He hadn't gone near the house, as he didn't want to hear that wife of his scoring him off. He was hungry and his stomach was churning. There seemed to be lights going off and on in his head and a shaft of heat seemed to stab through him.

Earlier – how much earlier he couldn't remember – he had seen his wife pushing the wheelchair down the lane. He scowled trying to remember. Oh, yes – she had blamed him for her having the toothache. He shook his head and it seemed as if a thousand pin pricks stabbed at him. Ben groaned to himself as his wife had said she was going to the doctors.

What good had doctors ever done for him? They had lectured him and never cured his son and had let his wife miscarry two of their children. After all, they made a good living out of people. Oh what the hell, he began to make his way back to the house where he slumped into a chair and thought bitterly about his thankless wife.

Jenny Briggs crossed the road as she got off the bus and made her way towards a café. Behind the counter, a pleasant woman smiled at her and asked her what she would like. Jenny asked for a cup of tea and then turned to the woman.

'Could you tell me if there is a family called Carter in the village? I used to know a Ben Carter and his wife years ago so I thought I'd give them a call since I'm in the district.'

'Oh, you probably mean the couple with the smallholding,' the woman smiled.

Jenny nodded.

'That'll be right. Ben always worked on the land.'

The woman went on.

'Such a nice person, Mrs Carter, and what a lovely girl young Iris has turned out. Oh yes, their daughter is a credit to them.'

She leaned over the counter and lowered her voice.

'Such a pity about the boy. Young David must be a heartache to all of them. Mind you, he gets every attention… hardly a day goes by when his mother isn't pushing him to the village. Why, they were in here earlier.'

Jenny sat and drank her tea. Well, it certainly sounded as if she had found where Ben Carter and his family lived. It would be nice to catch them unawares and it would make her day to see him looking at her and comparing her favourably with his freak of a wife.

With her tea finished, Jenny took the cup and saucer back to the counter where she was shown the direction of the Carter's house.

The rain was falling heavily as Jenny made her way down the main road. It seemed an age before she came to the twisty lane. At last she reached it and walked towards the cottage ahead.

The door was open which Jenny couldn't explain, but a strange feeling surged through her. She felt creepy and shuddered. What was she doing here? Jenny shook her head. She'd come to see Ben Carter and to see him smile at her, wishing for the old days back again.

'Hello, anyone home?' She pushed the door further open and hesitantly entered the cottage. She knew someone was there and called again and this time heard a rough grunt. She went forward, pushed the door further and stared at Ben Carter.

Whatever she had expected, it wasn't this. Ben Carter had turned into an old, grizzly, twisted faced man. As his eyes fell on her, he didn't see Jenny Briggs, a nice enough woman he'd once known; he only saw a stranger who was looking at him as if he were not fit to see.

'What are you doing here and what do you want? I don't want anyone nosing in here.'

His face took on an even more threatening expression. He half rose out of his chair and shouted.

'Get out. Nasty stinking bitch, go, get out!'

Jenny ran and raced along the passage and out into the yard. In the lane, she saw a movement and realised someone was coming. They must be stopped – Ben Carter was mad, he'd called her a filthy bitch and tears of fright and deeply felt hurt ran down her cheeks.

As Rose pushed the heavy wheelchair up the lane, she saw a figure at the top. The figure rushed towards her but Rose had no idea who it might be. She presumed it must be a customer for fruit or vegetables. They'd have to come back as she wasn't up to customers today.

Gasping, Jenny tried to warn Rose of the madman up at the cottage. Rose shook her head. There was something familiar about the woman's voice and, as she stared at her, she realised she recognised her.

'Good heavens! It's Miss Briggs, isn't it?'

Jenny nodded and her voice had an odd urgent sound as she spoke.

'I'm glad somebody still knows me. Listen, you can't go up there - he's mad… tried to set on me, he did.'

Rose shook her head.

'Don't worry, I'm used to his tempers. Look Miss Briggs, please come back and have some tea with us. Ben's bark is worse than his bite. He doesn't really like people to call. Still, you are an old friend, so he can jolly well be civil to you.

As they pushed the wheelchair up the lane together, the hatred in Jenny's heart melted. This woman was treating her not only with kindness, but respect. In all of her life, no one had ever shown Jenny either of these and she tried to thank Rose. Stealing a look at the twisted face, she remarked gently.

'Your poor face. Whatever happened, did that brute Ben Carter do it?'

Rose tried to smile.

'No. Oh, dear you mustn't think that. Ben wouldn't hit me it's just, well, he isn't very easy to live with.'

Jenny didn't sound convinced.

'He sounds like his father did. I knew them all in the old days, his brother was... well, what we used to call *only eight pence to the bob*. You know, not all there.'

Rose looked at her son. Since his birth, Ben had as good as always blamed her for the way their child was. If he had once half blamed anything else, it had been the fact that during her pregnancy, he had beaten her. Never had he intimated any possible family trait, which could have been responsible.

By now they had reached the cottage where Jenny took hold of the wheelchair and stood behind it in the passage. Rose walked down to the kitchen and went in and, with a cry, ran to Ben's side. He was slumped in the chair and she realised at once that he was only half conscious.

Remembering how busy the doctor's surgery had been, and recalling the doctor's words about the epidemic of

Asian flu, which was spreading like wildfire, Rose rang for an ambulance.

Jenny watched as he was carried out. His last look at her was no different than it had been earlier. David was staring at Jenny. She looked back at him and felt a strange sort of kinship with him. The child was regarded as an oddity, as she was. This boy would never know real friendship with another and neither had she. All her life she had depended on others to give her work and, like this child, she could only hope that the human beings with whom she came into contact would hold out the hand of friendship and smile at her.

Rose watched in amazement as Jenny began to take off David's coat and scarf and as she did so, she spoke to David. At once, he responded to her. Rose could hardly believe it.

At last David was bathed, fed and safely in bed. He had rather a high temperature but Rose felt sure that a good night's sleep would put him right.

Both women sat in front of the fire waiting for Iris to come in for tea and Rose insisted that Jenny relaxed and made herself comfortable. Her face was feeling much better now, indeed, the swelling and closed eye had reacted to the injection at the surgery and now she was beginning to look more her old self.

She set the loaded tray down in front of Jenny then took hold of her hand.

'I'd like to thank you for being so gentle and kind to my son. It isn't everyone he takes to, you see. So many people scare him when they shudder and turn away.'

The eyes of the two women met and, for the first time in her life, Jenny saw gratitude and thanks in the expression of the other.

Jenny never knew what made her say what she said at that moment. She looked straight into the eyes of the woman who had known such sorrow with the man Jenny had always wanted. Now she was glad beyond words that he had never proposed.

Her voice was quiet.

'If you ever want a live-in person to care for David, please think of me. I'll tell you now... from time to time, I take a drink. I would never need a drink if I had someone to care for, someone who needed me. I'd care for that child as if he were my own.'

Rose smiled and her words were genuinely warm.

'Thank you, Jenny. I'm glad we're on first name terms and that we are friends at last.'

Jenny's voice was quiet but sounded the genuine regret which she now felt.

'I'm sorry about being so spiteful and nasty to you when you were pregnant. I was jealous and well, I'm really sorry now.'

Rose looked at the woman. Since leaving Newcastle, she had never given a thought to Jenny. No wonder she had hated her. Rose had come out of the blue as an interloper into Jenny's world, not only that but she had been given a place of prominence in that world and, as if that wasn't enough, had married the man Jenny had set her heart on.

Rose smiled and started to make tea, inviting Jenny to join them, as Iris would soon be home.

Looking at Rose, Jenny felt really welcome for the first time in her life. She smiled and nodded. Rose felt strangely glad of the company.

'Tell you what. I know you've just had a snack but there's plenty to go round. Would you like to stay to tea, a real high tea, I mean, could you manage a couple of grilled chops and new potatoes?'

Again Jenny nodded.

'On one condition... that I do my fair share of the work.'

As she stood up she agreed to do the potatoes and, with a nod and a laugh, Rose led the way into the kitchen.

The sound of running footsteps brought Iris in with a breathless caring.

'Hello, mum. How are you? Did you go to the doctors and what did he say?'

As Jenny looked at the vibrant girl in the doorway, she realised who it was she had seen reflected in the mirror of the shop that first day in Hexham.

The sight of Iris looking so like her mother had done all those years ago gave Jenny an odd feeling of resentment. It lasted only a moment, however, and just as quickly, it was gone. This teenager belonged not to the old world but to a new changing era called the swinging sixties.

The telephone rang and Rose hurried to answer it. From the bedroom came the sound of snorting and bangs, David was awake and Iris, followed by Jenny, went in to see him.

It surprised Jenny how lovingly Iris soothed her brother. David's eyes rolled from one to the other when suddenly he fastened his gaze on Jenny and flung his arms in her direction. He made little grunting sounds and Iris expressed her amazement.

'Good heavens, he's taken a real fancy to you. He never does that to anyone except mum and myself. It's his way of showing affection and trust.'

Iris quickly went to tell her mother of the latest change in David. Rose was replacing the telephone and as she turned, Iris flung her arms round her.

'Oh, mum... mum what is it? Is dad worse?'

Rose held her daughter for a moment then gently disengaged herself.

'dad is very ill, he's calling for me. I must go, darling. Will you be alright? I'll ask Jenny if she can stay until I get back.'

Chapter XIII

Iris told her mother about David and his almost instant acceptance of Jenny as one of them. It was with a feeling of relief when Rose heard that Jenny was only too pleased to stay.

As she got into the taxi, she wondered just what else fate had in store for her. It seemed an age since she had wakened in the early hours with what she had thought was toothache. As Rose was to find out, the day of momentous events was not over yet.

Since Eric was staying in town, Stan went home alone. When he arrived, he was shocked to find Cara still in her wet clothes. She had obviously been drinking a great deal. The gin and vodka bottles were almost empty and she was in a dazed state.

Stan decided to try and sober her up. It took quite some effort but eventually, he managed to get her on to her feet. As they staggered about, he spoke bitterly.

'Why, Cara? Why do you have to drink so much? How do you think I feel when our son sees you like this?'

Cara swayed in her tracks, her voice was slurred and she was a little breathless as she spoke.

'Our son? You are wrong... not our son. Oh, no. Never *our* son... *my* son, yes *my* son and *Eric's* son. You never knew about my lovely Eric... I loved him!...'

Her voice died away.

Stan could hardly take in what she was saying. Eric was not his son, but that was impossible. They'd been married for over a year when their child was born. Then he suddenly remembered that Cara had gone off with two friends for a holiday on the Norfolk Broads. He hadn't really minded as business had needed to be drummed up at the Works, and without a wife to rush home to, he'd done quite well. He had stayed late, met clients at night and had really made the order books look quite healthy.

Cara had gone for one week, but now he remembered, she had stayed for three. When Cara spoke again, she left him in no doubt as to the truth of her earlier mutterings.

'My Eric, the man who is my son's real father, is Swedish and I met him on holiday. Remember, you let your wife go away and you didn't care that I went with friends. That damned firm meant more to you than I did, so I paid you out and fell in love with Eric. He is my son's father, not you.'

Cara suddenly started to sway and her eyes took on a glazed look and her mouth went slack. Stan quickly helped his wife to the settee then telephoned for an ambulance, then looked at the woman who had just hurt him beyond measure.

He went to the bureau which Cara rarely kept locked as he had never been a snooper. He reached in to a back drawer and brought out a number of diaries and carefully selected two from the late forties and put them in his pocket. The ambulance arrived and Cara was carefully carried out. Stan followed them in his car and later, when his wife was safely admitted to ward five of Hexham General Hospital, he sat at her bedside and started to read.

Rose sat watching her husband. Lying there, he suddenly seemed pinched and small. His face had a much gentler look and Rose sighed as he looked so helpless. Ben stirred and Rose took his hand which she gently squeezed. He looked up at her and tried to smile. He lightly sighed almost as if, thought Rose fancifully, it were such an effort.

Ben Carter was making an effort as he felt such a weakling and it wasn't like him to feel so frail. He knew he was in hospital but felt that as long as Rose was there, it didn't matter. Nothing really mattered, just as long as Rose was always nearby. He wanted to look into those great eyes of violet gentleness then he could peacefully go to sleep. All he had to do was look at her and he would be content again.

With an even greater effort, he turned his head and saw his wife smile down at him. The pain in his chest eased and he felt the ache in his face slip away. Ben Carter, for the first time in many years, felt a gentleness creep over him. He returned the light pressure of his wife's hand and peacefully slipped from life.

A watchful nurse rushed over to the bedside to feel for a pulse. She turned to Rose and shook her head as she felt no beat. The screens were quietly pulled around and Rose, after a visit to the sister's office for a cup of tea, liberally laced with whisky, found herself out in the grounds. There was a taxi rank at the other side of the car park and she wept silently as she made her way towards it.

Stan Bailey sat like a man turned to stone. The diaries had verified everything his wife had so drunkenly told him. The words drummed at him and the pain was like a searing stab. He had loved Eric from the first moment he had seen him. There had never been any cause for doubt regarding the boy's parentage. Stan tried to fathom how it was he had never doubted that he was Eric's real father. The truth of it hit him as he sat there. Of course, who would not love an innocent child as Eric had been born with Stan and Cara as his parents. Had he known that he wasn't the natural father, he still felt in his bones that he would still have loved the boy. As it was, Stan sighed and felt grateful that there had always been a special love and rapport between father and son. He wondered if there was a technicality to confirm he was a father by name only. He rose out of his seat and smiled – it was an ill wind that blew no one any good.

As Stan looked down at his wife, he marvelled at the years of deception which each had practised against the other. She had her secret and he had his. She loved a long lost lover and he had found his long lost love. Life could indeed throw out a tangled web of loves lost and found. As he watched, Cara opened her eyes, gave him a half smile, heaved a long gentle sigh then quietly left the world behind.

From a distance he heard the words, 'I'm so sorry, Mr Bailey, we did everything we could.'

Stan looked across at her and quietly thanked her. The nurse became businesslike and invited him to go into the sister's office.

Later, walking through a tree-lined avenue towards the car park, he saw the figure of a women coming towards him. There was something familiar about her walk. She was crying and as she came closer, he realised he recognised her. He became hoarse and whispered, 'Rose.' She stared at him and her own voice sounded unreal. 'Stan, whatever are you doing here?' They looked at each other then Stan took her arm. 'Let's walk. I know it's still a little wet but the cool air is what I need at the moment.'

They fell into step as both unfolded the events of their day. Each gave to the other a gentle understanding and quiet comfort which was a balm to them both. Stan explained to

Rose of his fears of that morning when he had discovered the growing feelings between Eric and Iris, how Cara had later told him, and how he had found proof in her diaries, that Eric was his son in name only. Whilst the knowledge had pained him, it had also saved them the difficult job of explaining how it was that Iris and Eric could never marry. That problem no longer existed.

Stan took Rose home and returned to Hexham after ensuring that she was safely indoors. He had a job to do and it wasn't going to be easy. He knew Eric would take the news of his mother's death very badly. It would be a doubly heavy blow due to its unexpectedness.

When he entered the house, it felt cold and smelt of gin. Stan quickly lit a fire and threw out the half empty bottles then sprayed air freshener round. Then, he carefully took all the diaries from the bureau and made an even more cheerful blaze in the grate. Stan had no wish to add more sorrow to his son than he had to. If, in the future Eric discovered the truth, it would sound much better coming from Stan himself than if he read those torrid old diaries. Stan poured himself a liberal whisky and sat down to await Eric's arrival.

Iris hurried to meet Rose as she entered the front door. The expression on her mother's face told all that was necessary. Having cried and comforted each other, they sat down to talk. There would be changes, there were arrangements to be made and strangely enough, Jenny became part of them.

When Rose suggested that Jenny stay the night, she gladly accepted. Rose told her that the back bedroom was small with a low beam across it but, nevertheless, she was most welcome. Jenny spoke earnestly.

'With this kind of trouble, you'll have a lot of running about to do. I'd like to help, I'd be glad to look after David and do a little around the house.'

Her voice took on an eager note.

'No need to worry about my employers, I'll put in a sick note and, if you like, I can stay until after the funeral.'

Jenny wondered how it was that she had ever disliked this warm, loving woman when Rose put her arms around her. She was now doubly determined to help the family in any way she could. She hoped that David would continue to accept her, as a strange communion had started to develop between them and she was sure that the boy cared for her, as indeed, she had come to care for him.

There was a great deal of running about to do before the funeral could take place and there had to be a post-mortem. The findings were pretty much as the doctor had told Rose to expect: Asian flu, allied to a slight stroke, had taken Ben Carter from the land of the living.

The funerals of both Cara Bailey and Ben Carter took place in the quiet little churchyards of Hexham and Rigton. An unspoken agreement between Rose and Stan meant that they would not meet for a while as each had thoughts and memories which needed a special kind of solitude.

The closeness between Eric and Iris continued to grow. Each comforted the other in the loss of a loved parent. Miss Pierce, who had now been informed of the circumstances of Eric's birth, sighed in sorrow for her beloved employer, but relief that the problem of her *dear children*, as she termed the two young people under her eagle eye, was now resolved.

It was late October when David became ill. In the night, his temperature suddenly shot up. Rose frantically called the doctor who, having taken one good look at his patient, immediately admitted him to Hexham General Hospital.

Never did a child have such devoted watchers – his mother, his sister and Ni-Ni. This was the nearest he had ever managed for anyone. Jenny firmly believed that the love she had carried for the boy's father, and which had been so cruelly rejected, had indeed been gladly accepted by his son.

As dawn appeared, David slipped peacefully from life. The Asian Flu had claimed yet another victim. He was buried beside his father in the little churchyard, which was full to overflowing.

As the sad little party left the graveside, an elderly man came and touched Jenny on the arm. It was the gardener from the local park. On many occasions when Jenny had taken David for his trip round the lovely floral walks, Old Joe, as he was affectionately known by everyone, had taken it upon himself to point out his special blooms and magnificent arrays. He held out a small bouquet and handed it to Jenny.

His voice was gentle as he spoke.

'I'll miss seeing the boy in the park. However, Jenny, I hope you'll still come as I wouldn't like to be missing both of you – please say you'll come.'

Thus it was that Jenny, having kept her promise some two months later, married a man who was to give her peace and happiness for many a long year. It was a delighted Jenny, who with her happy, gentle husband, decided to visit her sister.

At the turn of the year, Rose sold the cottage and the smallholding and with the proceeds, she bought an elegant town house on the outskirts of Newcastle called High Copperas Lodge.

It gave an extra special thrill to Jenny to be able to tell her sister that she would be staying the weekend at the lodge. 'You see Joan,' she gleefully informed her sister. 'The new owner is a special friend of mine. I was married from her lovely farmhouse in the country.'

Jenny had changed, but not entirely.

Yet another April came showering in and as it did so, Rose, for the first time in decades, did not weep. The tenth of April dawned with a hint of damp mist and Rose felt her heart sing.

It sang because it was her wedding day.

The years of trials and tribulations which had affected them both so tragically, were now just a distant memory.

Miss Pierce was overjoyed to find herself so much a part of this real life drama. When Rose had asked her to be bridesmaid, along with Iris, she demurred at first.

'I'm much too old for such a thing.'

Iris had put her arm round her and whispered.

'Dear Miss Pierce, where would we all be without your guiding hand to keep us right? Of course you must be bridesmaid. After all, you are like one of the family.'

Miss Pierce started to cry then finally, happily agreed.

The wedding was to take place in the little old parish church of High Copperas. Rose contacted her old friend Letty who was glad to hear of the good fortune which had come their way. A pools win had lifted them from near poverty to a comfortable living and they now owned a shop in the village and their three sons were at university. Letty was delighted when Rose asked her husband, Tom, to give her away.

The two bridesmaids, together with Letty, Jenny and Joe, swept out of the drive and down to the little church. It was, indeed, a gathering of friends, old and new, who came to see Rose married.

'You may kiss the bride.'

The words hung like a prayer above them and Stan turned and kissed his wife. Later, having signed the registers, the happy pair walked out into the April sunshine. The mist had vanished and the damp pathways were a myriad of dancing colours. Across the sky, a great rainbow arched a welcome, and with joy in their hearts, husband and wife walked towards it.

About the Author

Moya Mayo was born in the hungry thirties in Crawcrook, on the banks of the River Tyne. As a child during the Second World War, she kept the young children of the family entertained by reading her own stories and poems. Since the age of seven she has wanted to write a book of her very own. With a busy life as a working mother, in the 1980s she still found time to become interested in writing books for the blind and her stories gave enjoyment to many when they were heard on AIRS, the talking books network for blind people in Gateshead.

At nearly 80, she enjoys family life and writes stories for her grandchildren. Her hobbies include ballroom dancing and crown green bowls. *Rainbows in April* is Moya's first published novel and reflects the reality of life and love during the war years, which she lived through as a child and young adult.

Thanks to Ruth Askey – whose dedication to the production of this book must be acknowledged.